FLYING WITH THE EAGLES III

FLYING
WITH THE
EAGLES III

SOARING EVER HIGHER

Mary Trask

XULON PRESS

Xulon Press
2301 Lucien Way #415
Maitland, FL 32751
407.339.4217
www.xulonpress.com

Printed in the United States of America.

ISBN-13: 978-1-5456-7864-0

DEDICATION PAGE

This book is dedicated to all those called to a destiny much bigger than they could ever imagine. Though fear and hopelessness may attempt to thwart and divert them elsewhere, they choose to believe and trust the One who says they can succeed. By following the light, they will discover the truth and their gifted abilities to accomplish all that they were designed for from the beginning.

ACKNOWLEDGEMENTS

A s I worked my way through this amazing story, I need to thank several people who encouraged me throughout this labor of love. First, my amazing husband, John, who allowed me the many hours I needed to write down what I was seeing. As he read through this third book, he offered his honest opinions, discovered missing words, and then encouraged me to continue writing so he could find out what was going to happen next. I love that!

My great appreciation also goes out to all those who were excited and moved after reading my first two books in this trilogy. Their comments and encouragement greatly touched my heart as I saw the impact of this story upon their lives. I am so grateful for them all.

My dear friends, Dori Olson and Betty French, spent many hours with me as we edited and made corrections to help better convey this story so others could see this adventure as I did. I couldn't have accomplished this without their help. My thanks also goes out to our artist, Sam Wall (www.samwall.com) who worked hard to capture the look we needed for this third book.

Thank you all so much!

TABLE OF CONTENTS

Chapter One

A BACK-UP PLAN

Hooded figures from all over the island filed into the darkened room. room. Chatting nervously, they each found an empty chair in anticipation for the meeting to begin. Hamah himself was about to make an important announcement. He was known and recognized by all the village elders as one who had perfected and improved their ability to maintain control over others. Having him as their guest was a great honor. The elders were excited to hear his latest discoveries and newest methods from years of experimentation and research.

With only a blazing fire burning behind them for light, the chief village elder finally stood to his feet calling the elders to attention.

"Gentlemen! Welcome to you all," he began. "I am so glad you were able to join us. We have many important things to discuss this evening. The highlight of our gathering is a visit from our renowned benefactor from Camp Coshek where important research has been taking place. I would like to start the meeting by introducing Sir Hamah, our special guest."

Wild applause broke out as the white-haired man stood up, bowed, and then stepped up to the rough podium which had been provided. Placing his stack of papers in front of him, Hamah briefly thanked those who had invited him to come.

"Good evening, gentlemen. I have been asked to update all of you on the progress we have achieved at Camp Coshek. As you know, this camp was established many years ago to house and take advantage of our workforce coming from various prisons around the island. At first the imprisoned dissenters were simply forced into hard manual labor for the remainder of their lives. Some of you may know this work included chopping down trees, cutting firewood, and then feeding logs into the smoldering fires we have created to keep Kumani in the smoky haze we desire." Hamah continued.

"With these smoldering fires, we have been able to create the impression that Kumani is volcanic and could erupt at any time. Fear and the desire to survive has worked well to convince the populace that only with the careful oversight and direction of village elders will our society be able to survive. This plan has worked well for many generations—until now."

With that comment, many of the elders began ranting among themselves trying to figure out what Hamah was insinuating and if he was about to offer a solution as well. Hamah did not keep them waiting long.

"I am referring to the recent increase of escaping dissenters without success in recapturing any of them. From my notes here, I see that these dissenters are from various villages and have apparently joined forces. This is not good! Especially when I hear reports of other villagers viewing these dissenters as a type of hero. If this was to continue... well, you can imagine the chaos and trouble we might be facing as a result of this rebellion."

Again, the men burst out in anger each accusing the other of not doing his job efficiently enough. The volume of the crowd increased until the chief village elder quieted the group so Hamah could proceed.

"Gentlemen, I can see you are all very upset with my recent report, however, the good news is I do have a back-up plan. It should bring the people once again into proper submission. Before I divulge my plan, I would like to share my research."

"Throughout the many years of forced labor at Camp Coshek, I have been able to experiment with a number of plants growing on this island. One plant in particular carries with it an ability to cloud the mind so completely that people consuming it on a regular basis become unable to make decisions for themselves. After researching various blends of similar plants, we have learned how to dominate a man's thinking to the point where he or she will do whatever they are told with no questions asked."

An eruption of queries burst from the village elders wanting to know more about these plants and where they

3

can get them. Hamah held up his hands indicating he needed to continue, so the men quieted down to listen further.

"Before you get too excited about these plants, let me tell you, if not used in proper amounts, the effects can be devastating. Some of our experiments ended up with people reacting very badly and dying before we could use this concoction the way we wanted to. Since that time, we have perfected the amounts and now have in our service an army of former dissenters who will go anywhere and follow any direction we give them without question. This new army can now be used as an impenetrable force to back us up."

Applause erupted from the elders. They were thrilled with Hamah's new advances in research.

"Thank you, thank you," he responded before continuing. "The only key to maintaining our control over these enforcers is that they must be provided with a regular source of these toxins. This has been achieved by adding it to their water. In addition to this, we have also learned how to add some plants to our fires which add poisons to the smoke our residents are breathing. These toxins cause the people to become more tranquil and less clear-minded, which, of course, works to our favor. As you know, we regularly ingest medicinal herbs protecting us from the effects of these pollutants."

With nodding heads, the elders encouraged Hamah to proceed.

"With much discussion between myself and the other researchers, we have come to the conclusion that in order to help reestablish submission among our villages, an incident must be created. This will help renew the fears of the people and cause them to come running to us for 'protection and direction,' just as they have in past generations. We have come to the conclusion that the only thing big enough to scare our residents would be the utter destruction of a village by fire."

Rather than applauding this time, the elders sat stunned. One man had the courage to stand up to express his concern.

"What do you mean by 'utter destruction?'" he asked. "Our friends, families, and businesses are all located in our villages. No one wants to see that kind of destruction." Some of the elders stood expressing their agreement with his statement. Once more, Hamah raised his hands, quieting the crowd so he could finish. With an undertone of murmuring still present, Hamah proceeded.

"I understand your concerns, but let me explain the necessary purposes behind this. As the village burns down, we will be able to point to the dissenters as the responsible parties for this destruction. This will give us the excuse to increase our efforts in capturing them by releasing our new enforcers. This army will not hesitate in their pursuit, even when it comes to descending the smoking mountains, which is where we suspect the dissenters have gone. Once they are captured and properly disciplined, the people will settle back down into the lifestyle we have trained them in, just as we all desire."

Only a few of the elders applauded at this point. Another man stood to ask more questions.

"So regarding the burning down of one of our villages, how will we keep the people from revealing it was not the dissenters who burned the village down, but our own enforcers?"

"Oh, that is easy to take care of," Hamah responded. "No survivors."

"What? Are you suggesting we allow our friends and family to perish in this fire?"

Smiling, Hamah reassured them. "Oh, most of you won't have to worry about that at all. We have already selected one central village that will have the greatest impact upon the people."

"And which village is that?" another elder shouted from the crowd.

"We have selected the village of Yashen for this privilege," he announced.

"Wait a minute!" one elder shouted. "That is my village and my home! I did not agree to that!"

"Of course you didn't," Hamah replied. "This has been decided for you."

"There is no way I am going to allow that!" he declared.

"We figured that might be the case," Hamah responded coldly. "That is why we have brought some of our new enforcers to help you accept this decision."

Turning towards the entrance, he nodded at the men who had been waiting outside. Four enforcers entered the room and grabbed the one elder claiming Yashen as his home. The elder yelled and fought back, but was no match for the trained enforcers who quickly exited the building with him. Smiling, Hamah turned back to the remaining elders, some of whom were standing in shock.

"See? Problem solved. No survivors."

Chapter Two

A NEW HOME

The four friends, exhausted from their journey, watched in awe as the doorway to the mysterious Eagles' Nest opened before them. Clean sweet air filled their lungs-bringing refreshment and renewed strength to their weary bodies. Shoshanna and the others scanned the region taking in the splendor of the vibrant colors and aromas embracing them. Immediately on their left a roaring waterfall cascaded over the jagged-edged cliff above them.

Mists of moisture greeted them and brought life to mosses and ferns adorning the railed path which led down the steep wall into the peaceful valley below. With the thunderous waters so close, there was little they could say to be heard, so the group simply pointed at the sights as they maneuvered their way downward.

They took turns drawing attention to the elaborate cottages set along the winding roads below them. A huge guarded bridge lay on the far side of the massive village which was surrounded on either side by a wide river. They could see people moving along the roads going from structure to structure, but the largest of all the buildings appeared to be a meeting hall of some type. As they looked back at the waterfall, a glistening rainbow displayed radiant blues, reds, and greens in the bright sunlight shining down upon them.

The clarity and freshness of the whole region took their breaths away!

Galen, Shoshanna, Roany, and Uri had only walked half of the distance to the valley when one resident came to greet them.

Brushing aside his blonde hair, the man confidently stepped up to the travel-weary group and smiled warmly. Before he even spoke, they saw he was a strong, well-trained warrior who easily climbed the steep trail to greet them.

"Welcome, welcome, my friends! We are so excited to see you have arrived. Chen has told us much about you! My name is Azriel. I am to be your guide, helping you settle in before we begin your training."

While Azriel became acquainted with all the travelers, there was one in particular that caught his attention: Shoshanna. Though a little dirty and tired from her journey, the beautiful young woman with her long, braided chestnut hair and darkly lashed hazel eyes emanated beauty and strength both within and without. Her quiet confidence intrigued him.

"Training?" Roany spoke up. "Wasn't the entire journey here our training?"

"Well, your journey here was the prerequisite for you to begin your real training," Azriel explained.

"And what are we training for?" Galen inquired.

"I guess you could call us 'freedom fighters' as we learn the way of the eagle which brings freedom to all the residents. You realized this is the Eagles' Nest, right?" They all nodded in assent as he continued. "Well, just as the young eaglets train to fly and are then pushed out of the nest to be on their own, we are preparing to accomplish what we were each designed for among our own people."

"You have arrived at a very busy time as the first group of our warriors are getting ready to be sent out soon. We have been preparing for this season for quite some time," he added. "You will need to be trained so you can be dispatched as well. We have heard that Chen may be calling a special gathering soon to give us further direction."

Puzzled, Shoshanna attempted to understand more clearly. They had only just arrived and already Azriel spoke of sending them somewhere else.

"Does that mean, we won't be living here?"

"No. You will each have a permanent place here to live, but will be sent out on strategic assignments from time to time." Azriel responded.

Uri found the title of "freedom fighters" quite intriguing. "So, as freedom fighters, we have the opportunity to fight and conquer those opposing us? That could be fun!"

"Our enemy in this battle cannot be conquered by human effort, but rather this fight is in a whole new realm which we will shortly introduce you to," Azriel explained. "May I now escort you to the Hub for further instruction to help you get settled in?"

"Yes," Galen responded. "We are ready to begin!"

Following closely behind Azriel, they wound their way down to the bottom of the mountain. Once at ground level, the group was escorted into the Hub, a large building with a number of rooms and hallways jutting off the main lobby. Bustling around them, people of all ages, from young teens to the elderly, moved from room to room as if they were receiving something from each location.

"What is all this commotion about?" Shoshanna asked.

"We are getting ready to launch our first group to reach the villages of Kumani," Azriel explained.

"Do you mean 'launched' as sent flying through the air?" Uri questioned him. "That might be fun!"

Azriel had to laugh. "No. I'm referring to initiating a new effort on the island. As far as how residents get to their assignments, some walk to their locations, some are moved, while others are flown to where they need to go."

"Flown?" This puzzled Uri immensely. "Can people fly here?"

Amused by the questions, Azriel explained, "To be more accurate, I should say some of our residents are taken to their locations on the back of one of our eagles. I'm sure you noticed them when you entered into the canyon, right?"

"Oh yes," Uri assured him. "We definitely noticed them! At first, we thought we might have been their breakfast!"

Azriel smiled reassuringly. "No, no! Those eagles are like our pets around here. They were probably just curious. If they notice someone approaching not led by the light, they would notify us immediately. They are really quite tame and love working with us."

"Do you remember Jessah telling us about her flight on the eagle?" Roany reminded them. "Now we're learning that others fly on eagles as well! Amazing!"

"That is impressive! As we traveled though the canyon, I could hear the eagles making some interesting noises," Galen recalled. "It almost sounded as if they were speaking with each other. Do they do that?

"Oh, yes! They do communicate with each other," Azriel replied. Realizing the questions were only beginning, he interrupted them before they asked any more.

"Okay. I know you have a lot of questions about the Eagles' Nest. Many of them will be answered in our Introductory Training which is where I would like to take you now. Follow me."

As the group moved down the hallway, Azriel slowed his pace a little allowing him to walk beside Shoshanna. Leaning over towards her, he spoke in a low voice so only she could hear him.

"If we have time, maybe I can take you flying on the back of one of the eagles. This is something we all need to master at some point, anyway. It really is quite thrilling."

"Oh, I would love that!" Shoshanna replied.

"Great! We can see if this works out after you begin your instruction," he said, smiling.

Galen, who was not far behind, noticed the little inter-change between Shoshanna and Azriel. As he watched, something new rose up within him. "*Who does this man think he is?"* he asked himself. *"We have been through so much together and here he is showing off and making her laugh!"*

Not accustomed to being in a place where men pursued women, he wondered if he could hold Shoshanna's interest if she had others to choose from. His heart sank as these questions filled his mind.

Noting Galen's scowl, Roany came alongside his friend to encourage him. "Hey, we only just arrived here. Give Shoshanna a little time to adjust. I'm sure she will remember you and all we have been through together."

"I hope so," Galen replied, a little unsure. "I know I have to let her decide for herself. With all these changes, I hope she is still interested in getting to know me better. There are so many new people around, she might not be so inclined."

"No worries, my friend," Roany said while patting him on the back. "I mean look at those big strapping arms, muscular legs, and your ruggedly handsome looks! Who could ever forget you?"

Galen just shook his head laughing, though deep inside he knew this was in Elemet's hands at this point. With both single men and single women in this community, adjusting to freedom had now become the newest challenge they faced.

Chapter Three

UP IN ARMS

The old woman shook in anger as she listened to Yona's report. "How dare they put a twelve-year-old child's name on the list of 'available young women!'" she fumed. *"Wait until I get my hands on whoever is responsible,"* she told herself. *"I will let them know what I think of this foolishness!"*

Even as she raged at this injustice, a new strength and courage rose within her, something she had never felt before. Rather than the quiet submission she had lived under for so many years, she realized that it was time to act, not recoil.

"Yona, can you get me my shawl and cane, please?" Ms. Bina asked.

Startled at her request, Yona stood silent for a moment before responding. She had not seen Ms. Bina take one step outside the cabin since she arrived. Limited by her blindness, Ms. Bina did little more than sit in her chair during the day and sleep in her bed at night.

"Ms. Bina, are you sure about this?"

"I am! I refuse to sit here and do nothing as those ridiculous village elders take more and more privileges with no one holding them accountable! Someone has to speak up about this injustice!"

Seeing Ms. Bina's resolve and determination, Yona retrieved both her cane and shawl as requested. Once she returned with the items, the woman allowed the young girl to wrap the shawl over her shoulders and place the cane in her hand.

"When we go, child, I need you to hold my hand so I can see whatever Elemet wants me to see, especially in that print shop. I am determined to sort this out. Can you lead me there?"

"I can do that."

"And you just let me do the talking for you. Okay?"

"I will," Yona assured her.

Keeping a close eye on her footing, Yona led Ms. Bina through the center of the busy marketplace in their village of Chana. Local villagers wandered through the various shops purchasing ripened fruit, vegetables, and assorted fresh bread. To Yona, this had become a familiar sight, but she wondered how Ms. Bina would respond to all the new activity around her.

A new passion arose within Ms. Bina that Yona could clearly see. This once sedentary woman, content to sit and merely converse with others, was now moved to action as she determinedly placed her cane in the dust while they walked. Amazed by her transformation, Yona escorted her to the print shop as requested. As they drew closer, with

15

Yona still gripping her hand, she could tell Ms. Bina was already seeing things only Elemet could reveal.

Earlier that day, Yona herself had confronted the chubby man comfortably sitting behind the counter in the print shop when she discovered her name posted on the list of available young women. After speaking with Cobar, the owner of the print shop, she was even more distraught to discover that her name on that list was not an error as she supposed. Instead, he informed her it was a clear decision made by the village elders.

Though her "adopted" grandmother was quite elderly, she felt great relief seeing someone willing to stand up for her against this immoral injustice. She had no idea what Ms. Bina could do or even if her complaint would help at all.

Prior to their arrival, Ms. Bina reminded the girl not to let go of her hand when they stepped inside the shop. Yona nodded in agreement as the bell announced their arrival.

Recognizing Yona from her earlier visit, Cobar was curious about the elderly, blind woman she returned with. He stood up from behind his desk to greet them. With memories of that terrifying village elders meeting the night before still fresh in his mind, he was not about to let an old woman and a young girl bully him.

"Ah, Yona!" he smirked. "I see you have returned with a friend. What can I do for you?"

Ms. Bina exploded with fervency.

"You sir, can tell me how a twelve-year-old child's name could be added to the list of available young women for marriage?" she demanded. "I want to speak to whoever is responsible for this decision! They have gone too far!"

"Ma'am, I am sorry you feel this way, but according to the paperwork I have here, Yona, though a bit young, has met all the availability requirements, allowing her name to be added to the list," he stated while turning pages in a volume before him. "And who are you?"

"My name is Ms. Bina. I have resided here in Chana for many years. My late husband was Yanis, one of the doctors serving the villages in our area. As one of the leading residents, I demand to know what requirements you are speaking of and who is making these decisions for the young women in our village!"

A little surprised at her intensity, Cobar responded calmly. "Ms. Bina, may I remind you that the village elders have made these types of decisions for many years, not only for young women but also for the young men. Each of them is placed in a job and apprenticeship to secure our ability to survive and thrive on this island. Now, why are you speaking on behalf of Yona?" he inquired.

"Yona lives with me." she retorted. "As you can see, I am blind and having this child with me is very important!"

"Well, according to my records, I see here she is an orphan," he stated while pointing his finger at a location in the volume of records. "As an orphan, I would think placing her with a husband and giving her a permanent home would be a good thing! Let me assure you, another orphan can easily be secured to help you around the house."

"I don't want another orphan!" she responded as her voice increased in volume. "Yona has become like family to me and I am not about to stand by while some village elder decides she should marry at twelve years old! I demand to speak to an elder right now!"

Though angry, Cobar used great restraint to keep from revealing his own role in Yona's selection.

"Ms. Bina, might I remind you again that this is how things have been done for generations. Just because it is not convenient for you to replace Yona with another orphan, I see no reason for you to become upset enough to challenge a decision made by the village elders. I know at your age and especially with your obvious disability, you wouldn't want to become a dissenter! Though your deceased husband did hold a position of esteem in Chana some years back, this would not protect you from judgment before the elders should you be deemed a dissenter. You do recall that things seem to go very badly for dissenters around here."

Ms. Bina felt Yona's quick squeeze upon her hand, reminding her not to say too much. It was time for them to find another way to deal with this. Taking a breath to help calm herself down, Ms. Bina decided, rather than confronting this mindless puppet, she needed to take this concern to a much higher authority.

"Well, I wouldn't want to get myself into too much trouble over this, I guess. Maybe you are right. We have been doing things this way for generations. I really don't want to upset the elders, especially at my age. It appears there isn't too much I can do about this right now. I guess I just have to accept another orphan when that time comes," she feigned in defeat. "How much time do I have before Yona's presentation?"

"It looks like you have a month," Cobar replied, still burning at the audacity of even questioning the decisions of the elders. "The village elders will make sure a replacement orphan will be supplied shortly afterward."

"I am sorry to lose her, but I suppose I will be fine."

Still clutching Yona's hand, the two stepped outside to walk back to the cabin. As they walked away, Ms. Bina muttered quietly to Yona.

"It is a good thing you reminded me to hold my tongue. I was ready to whack that man on the side of his head with my cane! Oh, he makes me so mad, I could spit!"

"He said I only have a month!" Yona exclaimed, still in shock over the recent changes.

"Not if I can help it!" Ms. Bina responded. "I may be old and blind, but I am not ignorant. I can see what is going on here!"

"Did you see some things while we were in that shop?"

"Oh, I certainly did! That Cobar is one of the village elders and apparently his son is Zelig. Zelig wants you, so Cobar added your name to the list."

"What?"

"I told you Zelig was a snake!" Ms. Bina replied.

"Ms. Bina, I don't want you getting in trouble on my account," Yona stated.

"Not to worry child. I have lived in this village for a long time and have many friends."

19

"Yes, but how is that going to help us?"

Smiling, Ms. Bina continued. "It has been a while since I have seen some of my friends. I think it's time for us to plan a tea party."

"A tea party?"

"Yes. I think that is a lady-like thing to do. This will be a party unlike any I have ever given before. Come, Yona. Let's hurry home. We have much to arrange."

Once Ms. Bina and Yona exited the print shop, Cobar called for his son.

"Zelig!"

The back door to the print shop swung open as Zelig stepped in.

"Did you hear that?" Cobar asked, obviously irritated.

"Yeah, I heard it. Ms. Bina sounds like a fighter."

"Yes, and I thought you said Ms. Bina was just a blind, old lady who knew nothing," Cobar reminded him. "She may be a problem if we don't handle this right. I definitely don't want that Hamah to hear we are not managing our village correctly or he might be inclined to burn our village down as well. We need to squelch this, and quickly!"

"You're still keeping Yona on the list, right?"

"Yeah, but we'll have to keep a close eye on that Ms. Bina," Cobar added. "Blind or not, she looks like the type that could get things stirred up. We don't need any problems with dissenters around here, especially with that Hamah sniffing around our affairs."

"Didn't she say she would accept another orphan?"

"Yes, but I'm not convinced," Cobar admitted. "She changed her attitude rather quickly, and I'm not sure she is really in agreement."

"Don't you have other ways to take care of trouble-makers more quickly?"

"Yes, yes, we do, but with that girl in the house, it makes it a little challenging to get that brew into place without being spotted. Ms. Bina's late husband used to help us with that until he had to be removed. He knew too much and slowly grew resistant to our ways."

"Yes, I think I remember that," Zelig replied. "Too bad. He made things much easier for you."

"We'll just have to watch how things progress with Ms. Bina. I'm sure that the other village elders will agree. We cannot afford to take any chances!" Cobar decided. "I hope you appreciate all the extra trouble I am going through to get that girl for you!"

"Oh, I do. Yona is definitely the one I want. Thanks, Dad!"

"All right, all right. Just get back to work!"

As Zelig returned to the back room, Cobar decided to do his own investigation on Ms. Bina and her "deceased" family members. He wondered if Tanzi had actually been correct in her report regarding Ms. Bina and her sister, Haddie. Silently, he set to work going through all the records of the citizens on the island of Kumani.

He still had suspicions about Ms. Bina.

Chapter Four

MOVING OUT

"Do you want me to go with you this first time?" Miss Haddie inquired.

"No. I think I will be fine," Jessah replied. "I'm just going to sneak into Malia's room and talk with her for a while before I come back. How about you? Are you going to visit Ms. Bina tonight like you planned?"

"Well, as long as you are comfortable with your visit to Camp Shabelle, I do plan on speaking with my sister so I can encourage her through the challenges she is facing," Miss Haddie answered. "She's new to the ways of the eagle and could use some additional wisdom."

With a twinkle in her eye, ten-year-old Jessah welcomed the opportunity to experience a whole new way of travel. As one who had already flown on the back of an enormous golden eagle she nicknamed "Goldie," the idea of stepping through a doorway to be transported to a new location sounded thrilling. Besides that, after living in Camp Shabelle for a number of years, she had great compassion for all the orphans currently stuck in the midst of their re-education process. This was her opportunity to help them.

"Will we both leave here at the same time and return at the same time?" Jessah inquired.

"I believe you leave here first and then I will follow. You might return before I do, so you can just go to bed and rest up when you get back. It could be close to dawn before we finish. My sister and I have a lot to discuss."

"Oren is still in the guest cottage, right?" Jessah checked.

"Oh, yes. He will be there all night. If you have any questions or concerns, we can discuss them tomorrow. Are you ready to head out?"

"Oh yes! I am so excited!"

"Okay, child. First close your eyes and then look for the archway which will appear before you."

As Jessah stood next to Miss Haddie with her eyes tightly shut, she moved her head around a little to look for the archway.

"I see it! I see it! The archway is right in front of me." she answered excitedly.

"Okay. So when you step through it, you will find yourself inside Camp Shabelle. Things will be quite dark there, but do use caution as people will be able to see you if you are moving around," Miss Haddie instructed her. "Once you are sure everything is clear, move directly to the girl's dorm where Malia is sleeping. Wake her very gently so she won't be alarmed. After that, you know what to do. Correct?"

"Yes, I know what I need to do."

"And when you have finished speaking with Malia, just return to the same place you started at, close your eyes, then step back through the archway."

"I understand."

"Then go ahead, Jessah. The light will direct you."

As Miss Haddie watched, Jessah took one step forward and disappeared from the cottage. Taking a breath herself, Miss Haddie also closed her eyes and took a step through the archway before her.

In a split second, she found herself in the darkened cabin where Bina resided with Yona. The rhythmic breathing of sleep filled their dwelling. Being careful not to make any undue noise, she quietly moved from the living room into Bina's room. Shutting the door to avoid disturbing Yona, she gently moved over towards her sister's bed patting her hand to arouse her.

"Bina," she whispered. "It's me, Haddie. Are you awake?"

At first, Bina just yawned, stretching before she spoke. "Is it morning yet?"

"No, it is still night. I was sent here to check in on you. I understand you and Yona are having some difficulties."

Suddenly Bina was wide awake. "Haddie! You have returned! Yes, please help me sit up, so I can discuss with you all that has transpired since our last visit."

Haddie assisted her sister in sitting up and then pulled two chairs together so they could discuss things freely. The two women spoke in soft tones throughout much of the night as they worked out the strategies needed to combat the evil plans of the village elders.

Meanwhile, after stepping through the archway in Miss Haddie's cottage, Jessah opened her eyes and found herself in a darkened hallway within the confines of Camp Shabelle. It had been quite a while since she had been forced to call this place her home. The familiar chill of the building caused Jessah to shudder as she acclimated to the colder temperature.

Taking a moment to remind herself why she was there, she scanned the area looking for that familiar light that had often led her through its dark and gloomy passageways. Once spotted, Jessah moved with confidence following its clear direction until she arrived at one of the dormitories for the girls.

With a slight creak, the door swung open allowing her to quietly slip inside. The room was filled with sleeping girls on every side. With no apparent way to determine which one was Malia, she decided to approach and study each of the girls faces until she found her friend. Fortunately, a full moon was shining through the large barred window adding some degree of visibility. Just as she was approaching the first sleeping child, she noticed the light had reappeared near a particular bunk bed.

As Jessah drew close enough to see, she realized the light led her to the right bunk and to the one she was looking for.

"Malia," she whispered. "Wake up, Malia. It's me, Jessah."

Slowly, the child turned and stretched a little before opening her eyes. Blinking for a moment, Malia didn't recognize Jessah at first, but as she stared, everything came back to her.

"Jessah!" she whispered. "You're back! Where did you go? It has been a long time since you disappeared... and not one of the grown-ups even noticed! How is that possible?"

Bringing her finger to her lips to remind Malia they had to remain very quiet, she beckoned her friend to follow her out of the dorm so they could speak freely. Quickly Malia grabbed her blanket, wrapped it around her shoulders, and followed Jessah to an area in the building where she was sure they would not be heard or discovered. The light made it very evident where they needed to go.

Once they arrived, Malia threw her arms around her friend.

"I am so glad you came back! You were the only one I could really talk to in this place... and then you disappeared! How did you do that?" Malia asked, quite puzzled about the whole thing.

"Malia, I don't really have time to explain everything right now, but I wanted to let you know I have not forgotten you, nor has Elemet. Do you remember me telling you a little about him?"

"Oh, I have thought about everything you told me almost every day in this terrible place."

"Well, I first want you to know Elemet has a plan for you and all the children here. I will be coming from time to time at night so I can train you in the ways of the eagle and then you can begin training the other children as well."

"Me? Elemet has a plan for me?" she asked in amazement that he would even be aware of her in this dark place.

"Yes, he really does! The only thing he asks is that you never mention his name or my name to any of the adults. They will have their own opportunity for a decision at another time. Right now, the focus is on you. Can you do that?" Jessah asked.

"I can."

"Good! We will meet once or twice a week at night as Elemet directs. Whatever I teach you, he wants you to share with the other children a little at a time. He will direct you to the ones to speak with first, and then they will speak to those he chooses for them as well. This way, the message can spread very quickly here. Understand?"

"Yes! So when you finish with me each night, will you disappear as you did before?" Malia asked.

"Yes. Miss Moselle and the other adults will have no idea I am visiting you at night. I will leave, and then you will watch for the light directing you to the child you need to speak with."

"I do understand. This is so exciting. It's like I am on a secret mission!" the curly-haired child exclaimed. "So tell me what I need to know! I can hardly wait!"

Slowly and clearly, Jessah explained the first step in her friend's training. Malia's blue eyes were wide with eagerness as she drank in the words like dry ground receiving the water it craves.

It was many hours before Jessah escorted Malia back to her bed. Though it was still dark outside, the haze revealed increasing light in the distant horizon. The girls hugged one more time before Malia climbed back into her bed and Jessah slipped out the door once again.

The sun was just beginning to shine as both Miss Haddie and Jessah stepped back into the cottage nearly at the same time! Though a little tired, each was able to give a quick account of her mission before retiring to bed.

It had been a most productive night!

Chapter Five

A NEW ASSIGNMENT

D iscouraged and disheartened by his failure with Galen's parents, Mendi kicked a few stones out of the way as he traveled down a very well-known trail leading to the village of Chana. He had heard the village elders say they might be able to use his assistance.

His handsome appearance and muscular build had always gotten him what he wanted in life. He had been a star pupil at Camp Shabelle and selected as a special trainee where he could put his good looks to use. His wavy brown hair and bright smile had succeeded in winning over even the most difficult of people as he obtained the information needed by the village elders. However, his failure in Kieran nearly blacklisted him throughout that region.

Eber and Giza, though old, had outsmarted him. Galen's father, Eber, had led him through the forest, drugged him with some concoction, and left him asleep in a remote cave forcing him to find his way back. When he did return, they were gone and their cabin was burned to the ground. His reputation as a successful plant and informant was left

29

in ashes, much like the charred remains of the old couple's home.

He hoped he might do better in the village of Chana. He had heard that the elders there were still looking for young recruits to scour the forests looking for the dissenters. Enforcers were paid generously if they included the region of the smoking mountains in their search. Though many had tried, none had succeeded in capturing the new "heroes" of the people. He had no interest in traipsing through the forest. He hoped that this new village might offer him the opportunity to befriend some new "victim" on behalf of the elders.

This is what he had been trained to do.

As Mendi drew closer to Chana, he happened to pass by a simple cabin on the edge of the village where a young girl was outside hanging linens on a line. She caught his attention immediately. Her glistening, long brown hair swayed behind her almost like a dance as she leaned over grabbing the next item to throw across the rope strung between two trees. Glimpses of her sweet face, though from a distance, caused his heart to race.

He needed to know who she was.

Walking up to her, Mendi smiled widely and spoke in his most charming manner hoping she would respond.

"Hi!" he called out as he moved closer to her. "I'm new in this area and wanted to see if this was the village of Chana."

She turned towards the stranger, briefly scanning him with her dark brown eyes to decide if she would even respond. Not really in a mood to chat, she tried to at least be cordial. "Yes, this is Chana. Are you looking for someone?"

Pulling a folded piece of parchment from his knapsack, he opened it and read aloud, "Cobar. I am looking for Cobar at the print shop."

"Oh," she barely responded before turning back to the linens in her basket. Mendi, not used to being ignored, ducked under the clothesline and reappeared directly in front of the young girl.

"Did I say something that upset you?" he asked.

She stopped and looked intensely at him once again. "I told you this was Chana, didn't I?"

"Yes, but why won't you tell me where Cobar and his print shop are located?"

A little annoyed at Mendi's persistence and the mention of Cobar's name, she tried her best to ignore him. If he was looking for Cobar, she suspected he might be an enforcer, or even worse, one of Cobar's new cohorts. He continued to press her for an answer. Finally, she snapped back.

"I want nothing to do with Cobar and his print shop!" With that, she turned away again to grab another of the linens. "I have work to do. You can ask someone else for directions."

Her spunkiness was intriguing. He had to continue.

"And why does this Cobar upset you so much?" Once again, the girl stopped to better examine this young man. Was he seriously interested in hearing what she thought about Cobar? Realizing he was not about to abandon their conversation until he had his questions answered, she decided to test him further.

"What does it matter to you?" she boldly replied. "You are probably working for Cobar, anyway."

"Honestly, I'm not yet working for Cobar. Is there something I need to know before I speak with him?"

"You wouldn't care," she replied while attempting to turn away.

"Try me!"

Looking deeply in his eyes, the girl thought she might have seen a glimmer of real compassion emanating from this persistent young man. She decided to tell him.

"Cobar and the village elders have added my name to the list of eligible young women to be presented next month."

"And what is so bad about that? Don't you want to be married?"

Stunned by his comment, the girl just shook her head and turned back to her work.

"I'm sorry," he quickly replied when he saw her response. "I guess I don't understand why getting married to someone is such a terrible thing. Since we have to be married at some point, I don't see anything wrong with having a young woman as beautiful as you selected for someone like me, for example. I wouldn't mind that at all!"

The girl had to smile a little at his compliment, but still, his ignorance and poor perception of the whole process amazed her.

"Thank you for the compliment, but you do realize that none of us have any say in the matter? Village elders choose whoever they want to be with whatever man they decide. Neither of us will choose anyone. It is all decided for us. They even decide when they think we are ready to marry!"

"Well, I'm not opposed to getting married. Are you?"

"I'm against getting married too young and being given to a man who has no respect for women at all… a man who only sees a woman as a possession and not as a real person."

"But what if the man does respect you and honors you as a person? That could happen, couldn't it?" he persisted.

Bowing her head for a moment before continuing, the young woman had to admit, some couples did seem to have a happy and productive life together, but in her case, the whole thing seemed hopeless.

"If you must know, Cobar's son has decided that he wants me as his wife… and I detest him! He and his father have arranged for my name to be added to the list, though I am only twelve years old! As an orphan, I have no parents to object, so the village elders do whatever they want, leaving me with no say in the matter. Does that sound fair to you?"

Mendi stopped for a moment to consider what she was saying.

"No, that doesn't sound fair or right," he admitted. "So, you are only twelve?"

"Yes, I want to enjoy being a child a little longer without being forced into adulthood. Only a short while ago I was still living in Camp Shabelle," she explained. "Before my twelfth birthday, I was sent here to help this sweet, blind woman who has become like family to me. She is the only family I have ever known! I don't want to leave and I don't

33

want to be married to that terrible Zelig!" she stated as tears streamed down her face.

Mendi had little to say to console the young woman before him.

"If you still want to go see Cobar, I can tell you where to go," she added through her sniffles. "I know this is not your fault."

After giving Mendi directions to the print shop, the young woman returned to hanging the linens as before. However, before leaving the area, he suddenly stopped in his tracks.

"Wait!" he said while walking back to her. "You didn't tell me your name."

"What difference does it make?" she replied. "My future has already been planned out by the village elders."

"Yes," Mendi replied, "but maybe our futures can be changed. You never know."

With only the slightest hint of a smile, she replied, "Yona. My name is Yona."

"Don't give up hope, Yona. There may yet be a way for you to choose your own destiny without being forced into plans others have made for you. I'm going to speak with Cobar about this."

"Oh, no! Please don't do that. I don't want to see you get into trouble as well. Others are already trying to help me."

"You know, I have already been in trouble before. I'm growing tired of doing only what others tell me to do. Maybe it's time for me to start thinking and deciding things for myself," Mendi said. "I am pretty good at making friends with people. Maybe I can win this Cobar over and learn what is really going on, so I could help you."

"Be careful," Yona warned. "These are not people to be trusted at all."

"I know. I am used to working with unscrupulous people," he smiled. Hesitantly Mendi added, "Would you mind if I come back to visit you? I could give you updates on what they are planning and maybe get to know you a little better."

"Yes. I guess so. Just don't let them know you are talking to me. They wouldn't hesitate in throwing you in prison if they suspected you to be a dissenter."

"I realize that. I'm actually not very proud of my past and maybe this would be a way for me to do something good for once. See you, later, Yona."

As he turned once again to walk into the village, Yona called out behind him.

"And what is your name?"

"Mendi!"

"Thank you, Mendi!"

Smiling, Mendi turned toward the village. This was the most peace he had felt in a very long time.

Chapter Six

NOT FORGOTTEN

The forest floor crunched under Oren's feet as he walked along the trail towards Eber and Giza's homestead. The early morning prompting he had received was clear. It was time to check on those he had been given charge over to see how they were adjusting. As he moved along, however, a nagging question continued to disturb him.

It appeared as though all the other people following the way of the eagle had amazing encounters with Elemet or Chen, while he had only Miss Haddie as his teacher. Was he not important enough to warrant an encounter of that type?

He recalled all the stories Miss Haddie shared describing experiences she had throughout her many years of living in this uncommon manner. Jessah, though young, had already experienced a number of things that almost made him feel jealous. Eber and Giza sat with Chen one evening as he explained their new mission to them. Even Tanzi, as new as she was to this uncommon lifestyle, spent hours with Chen while still blind. Her transformation after his visit was amazing.

"What is wrong with me?" he wondered. *"Am I not worthy of my own encounter? Maybe I haven't done enough for Chen and Elemet. Could it be my role as the woodsman means I will never have that kind of encounter?"*

Noticing the negativity of his thoughts, he decided to focus just on his assignments in the region to avoid discouragement. While hiking, Oren became aware of someone following him. Stepping behind a tree, he prepared himself to enter into that "safe realm" which hid him from any enforcers who might be roaming around. Before vanishing, he decided to wait a moment listening for any other sounds.

"Oren."

He nearly jumped out of his skin as he realized the voice was right beside him! Turning his head, he saw a man with glistening white hair and dazzling blue eyes standing right next to him. With no words of explanation, Oren knew exactly who it was.

"Chen!" he exclaimed, feeling a little ashamed as he realized he had been entertaining thoughts of jealousy and self-pity. "I didn't expect to see you," he fumbled out.

"I know that. Did you think I had forgotten you?" Chen asked.

"Oh, no!" he replied, but then changed his mind. In Chen's presence, facades were impossible as everything became clear and apparent.

"I guess I was entertaining negative thoughts about that," Oren admitted. "I'm sorry. It's just that everyone else has had these amazing encounters, and I couldn't help but wonder why not me?"

"Why don't we walk as we discuss this?" Chen suggested. Nodding, Oren stepped out from behind the tree. Chen continued.

"Comparison is a very dangerous thought to entertain. When we examine the lives of others, we forget about all the good that has been accomplished in our own lives," Chen reminded him. "Each individual has been created with unique gifts, abilities, and destiny. Achieving the distinct mission for every person requires different experiences and training to properly prepare them for what lies ahead."

"Your life experience has not been the same as Jessah's, has it?" Chen asked.

"No," Oren admitted.

"What about Tanzi? Is she a completely different person from you?"

"Absolutely."

"And are you the same as either Eber or Giza?" Chen continued.

"I'm not."

"And what about your daughter, Shoshanna?" Chen proceeded. "Is she exactly the same as you?"

"No. She is very different."

"Then, how could anyone assume their experiences as they progress in the ways of the eagle would be like anyone else's training?" Chen asked with a smile that assured Oren that he was never forgotten by the one who loved him.

"You're right," Oren responded.

"As my woodsman," Chen continued, "you may not see me all the time. However, this does not mean I am unaware of you. You are a key person on this island of Kumani whether you realize that or not. I am very present at all times and take great pleasure in watching your growth and progression. Your gift as an encourager has been very evident in the lives of those I have sent you to. Are you ready to continue your mission of mercy now?"

"I am ready," Oren answered.

"Good!" Chen replied, "You have arrived."

As Oren glanced around, he suddenly realized that he was just outside the perimeter of Eber and Giza's home. When he looked back to thank Chen, he was gone.

Stepping across the border, he was surprised to see how the homestead had grown even in the short span of time they had arrived. Fully ripened fruit hung from the trees growing around the boundary of their cottage, with lush vegetables and varieties of herbs flourishing everywhere. Even berry bushes with plump, sweet fruit ready to pick called out.

From the cottage, the scent of freshly baked bread beckoned him to hurry and knock on their front door. Both Giza and Eber happily greeted him as they invited their guest inside.

Though they had escaped the cabin with only meager supplies and a few pieces of furniture, Eber had been at work building a new table, chairs and other necessary items to make their new home very comfortable indeed. After examining their cottage, Oren offered his compliments to the couple for all they had accomplished. As a house-warming gift, he opened his knapsack and produced some venison, cooked chicken, and a fresh supply of Miss Haddie's special tea for them to enjoy.

Thrilled, Giza quickly set to work preparing a mid-day meal for them all. Fresh, warm bread with honey was set before the two men along with steaming cups of tea for them to enjoy while she gathered the foods needed for their lunch.

As Giza buzzed around the kitchen humming happily, the two men talked.

"While I was out gathering wood for our furniture, I noticed several young men wandering around not far from our homestead," Eber informed him. "They didn't see me and once I returned to the property, I noticed that the trees and bushes around us swelled up to protect us from discovery. There seems to be a lot more activity around these woods lately. Do you have any idea what is going on?"

"Not yet, however, I do intend to visit Tanzi to see if she knows anything," Oren replied.

"How is Tanzi doing now?" Eber asked. Though fully aware that Tanzi had been responsible for their son's arrest, after Chen spent time with them, he filled in some of her history for them, allowing the couple to forgive and release her from any offense. They had heard of her blindness, her change of heart, and knew she was awaiting further instruction.

"The last time I saw her, she was quite brokenhearted over all the trouble she had caused," Oren responded. "I'm sure Elemet has offered her more instruction in the ways of the eagle during my absence. My plan is to go visit her next. I do feel a sense of warning regarding her current location because of the easy access the village elders have to her right now. I can stop by on my return trip and let you know how she is doing, if you like."

"That would be great," Eber smiled. "Though she did betray us in the past, Roany and she were close friends, as our sons grew up together. Both Giza and I have quite a heart for her." Giza, overhearing their conversation, responded in agreement.

"Yes, Oren. Please let Tanzi know that we would love to see her sometime. We have too much of a history together to walk away from her."

"I will do that," Oren replied.

As the men continued discussing plans for the future, in short order Giza produced a wonderful meal for all of them to enjoy before Oren had to press on in his journey. Once the food was eaten, the couple offered some of their bounty to share with Tanzi. Gratefully, Oren accepted the food on her behalf, packed up his knapsack, and headed back out into the woods to continue his mission.

Even as he was leaving, he could feel a growing sense of concern for Tanzi. Something was going on and he needed to find out what. Increasing his pace, Oren moved toward the village Kieran.

Chapter Seven

ADJUSTING TO FREEDOM

After their first training session at the Eagles' Nest, Shoshanna, Galen, Roany, and Uri all felt as though their heads were spinning with all the new information they had been given. A history of the Eagles' Nest explained the "hows and whys" of this heavily protected region as they learned the great importance of replacing lies with truth. With the heavy indoctrination given throughout the lifetime of each resident on Kumani, it was necessary to remove every falsehood so that real clarity could be established in their minds. After clarity came the proper equipping necessary to combat the stifling haze that still filled the lowlands outside their region.

Upon exiting their first session, the friends were greeted by another resident, Talia, who was sent to lead them to their new rooms.

"Hi," she greeted them. "Welcome again to the Eagles' Nest. I'm here to take you to the rooms where you will be staying during your training. Have you enjoyed your introductory session this afternoon?"

"I don't know if I would use the word, 'enjoyed,'" Uri responded. "I feel as though my head is about to explode with all this new information."

Laughing, Talia promised it would get easier after hearing all the new information several times. The repetition would help them remember what they were learning. As they walked, she continued, "I can still remember my first days here as well. So much of that time was quite a blur."

"How did you happen to come here?" Shoshanna asked the young woman.

"Oh, I came here with my parents and younger brother several years ago," the fair-haired woman responded. Her hazel eyes sparkled as she recalled the moment they first stepped through the stone doorway overlooking the Eagles' Nest. "What a relief it was to discover this place actually existed just as we had been told."

"And what led your family to make the decision to leave the lowlands?" Galen inquired, quite curious to hear their motivation for such a difficult journey.

"My father was being forced to work long hours at the mill, and after witnessing a serious accident, he realized how little the village elders cared for the people," Talia explained. "He and my mother decided to find a way out before I was forced to marry someone of their choosing. That's when they met her."

"Met who?" Galen probed.

"Miss Haddie, of course! She is quite a celebrated individual around here," Talia reported. "Nearly everyone has Miss Haddie to thank for directing them to the Eagles' Nest."

"That makes perfect sense," Shoshanna responded. "She certainly was a lifesaver for me! I was desperate to find a way out of that lifestyle."

"As we all were!" Talia replied while approaching a large chalet-style building. "This first building is where Shoshanna will be staying with some other young women. We call it, 'Ashlene's Lodge' in honor of the first single woman who made the journey here."

"You already know my name?" Shoshanna asked in surprise.

"Oh yes! Chen kept us posted of your progress so we could prepare for your arrival."

"Of course he did," Roany commented. "Chen has quite a habit of appearing at important times!"

"He certainly does!" Talia laughed as she finished giving Shoshanna final directions on how to find her room and get settled into the lodge.

Meanwhile, Roany could not get his eyes off their beautiful guide. He hoped his companions had not noticed his stares. He wondered if he would get an opportunity to speak with her privately at some point. Attempting to appear nonchalant, he forced himself to look away as if he were studying the other buildings around them.

Uri, however, missed nothing when it came to young men with eyes for the ladies around them. Once Talia completed her instructions to Shoshanna, she led the men a short distance further to the lodge where they would be staying. Siding up to Roany, Uri stared at him with a huge grin until Roany could stand it no longer.

"What are you staring at?" he asked his friend.

"I can see what is going on here," Uri replied, still with a silly smirk across his face.

"Uri, what are you talking about?" Roany questioned him, acting as though he was unaware of anything unusual.

"You like her," he whispered while nodding his head. "I know you like her."

"Who?"

"Talia!" Uri responded as though he had just uncovered a hidden secret.

"Uri, stop it! We just met her. That is ridiculous!"

"I can see it in your eyes," Uri persisted. "Why don't you get closer so you can talk to her?"

"Look, Uri. We don't know anything about her. Maybe she already has someone special in her life. I don't want to make a fool of myself."

"I don't think anything is wrong with getting to know someone better," Uri encouraged him.

Suddenly, Talia noticed that Uri and Roany had dropped back, so she called out urging the two men to get closer to Galen so they all could hear her instructions. Roany glanced at Uri with a look of warning, hoping he would not say anything embarrassing in front of Talia as they quickened their pace.

Once they arrived in front of another lodge with the name "Shraga Chalet" painted in bright colors above the doorway, Talia stopped, indicating this was their new residence.

"So let me guess," Galen began. "This was named after the first man who made the journey here, right?"

"Actually, this chalet was named after my father who just completed a renovation on it," she smiled. "With more of you single men coming in, he had to add a wing with several new rooms. You three will be the first to stay in those rooms. I hope you enjoy them!"

"Thank you!" Galen responded as he moved to open the front door. As Uri stepped towards the door himself, he gave Roany a shove placing him right in front of Talia.

A little red-faced at Uri's forwardness, Roany searched for something to say.

"Do you have a question, Roany?" Talia inquired. Uri glanced back at him with a nod as he stepped through the front door.

"Well, actually I do," he admitted a little sheepishly. "What do people do around here to get to know someone better?"

"Oh!" she laughed. "That is a good question. Once a week, we have a special gathering in the meeting hall we call the Hub. This is where everyone is encouraged to learn more about those living here. Lots of food is provided as we visit. After a time, Chen gets up and gives us a detailed report on progress and challenges in the lowland. I'm actually hearing that there might be a special meeting with Chen sometime soon. You won't want to miss that!" she assured him.

"Well, great. I will definitely plan on that," he stammered as he moved past her towards the door.

"Roany!" Talia called after him just before he entered the chalet. Stopping in the doorway, he turned back to look at her. "I would love to get to know you better myself, if you'd like."

Surprised, Roany replied, "That would be great! I look forward to visiting with you there. Good night!"

"Enjoy your rest," she responded while spinning around towards her own home.

As soon as Roany entered the chalet, Uri was right in front of him. "Well? What happened?"

"Can we talk about this later?" Roany asked. "I'm pretty tired."

"Nope. Talk now. I want to hear everything," he said with a familiar grin, letting Roany know he was not about to let him change the subject. With eyes rolling, Roany filled Uri in with all the details. There was no getting away from it!

Chapter Eight

WHEN THE ENEMY COMES CALLING

A loud knocking on the front door caused Tanzi to jump while pouring hot water into her cup for tea. The seeping tea overflowed onto the table. Grabbing a cloth, she quickly wiped up the spill before answering the door.

She was not expecting anyone. Puzzled, she opened the door and was greatly surprised to see Zelig standing before her. The seriousness of his expression let her know this visit was purely business.

"Oh! Good morning, Zelig. Would you like to come in?" she asked in an attempt to be sociable. Knowing his status and connection with the village elders made her quite uncomfortable.

"I guess I can come in for a moment," Zelig replied. Gravitating towards the table where he spotted a warm cup of tea, he boldly walked over and picked it up. "Is this for me?" he asked even as he prepared to sip the warm, fragrant drink.

"Uh, sure! Go right ahead," Tanzi responded, though Zelig had already begun sipping the tea. "Can I help you with something?"

Waiting until he had swallowed several sips, Zelig finally answered, "My father wants to meet with you."

Once again, Zelig took several more sips of the tea while standing next to her table. Tanzi stood, puzzled by the request.

"Did he say why he wants to meet with me?" she asked.

"This is really good tea," he commented while hardly acknowledging her question. "Where did you get this? I think I'd like to have some of my own."

Perturbed by his lack of response, Tanzi replied, "It's a special blend given to me by a friend. Now can you tell me why Cobar wants to meet with me?"

"Do you think you could get some of this tea for me? I really like it."

"Yes, I will get you some tea!" she responded, obviously irritated with the young man. "Now please answer my question. Why does your father want to see me?"

Finishing the last of his tea before responding, Zelig replied, "He said he wants to know more about Ms. Bina. She lives in our village, you know. He recently had an encounter with her and wants to find out what you know about her."

"I reported all that I knew at the last village elders gathering some time back," she answered nervously. "There is nothing new to tell him."

"Well, you can tell him that to his face," Zelig retorted. "He wants you to come immediately so he can speak with you." Glancing down towards his empty cup setting on the table, he continued.

"Before we leave, do you have some of that tea you can give me now? Once you get it packed, we can leave and head towards Chana. My father is waiting," he said with a cocky smirk.

Irritation quickly changed to full out annoyance at the arrogance and indifference to the needs of others demonstrated by both Zelig and his father. Requesting an audience with someone was one thing, but this outright demand and their full expectation of immediate compliance left Tanzi stunned.

With her own mind cleared from the darkness and haze of the past, the outright control of others was now very evident. Silently, she cried out to Elemet asking for both sound wisdom and the grace she needed to deal with these dangerous men.

Addressing Zelig, she replied calmly, "I will need a few moments to gather up the tea you requested and then grab my shawl for the journey, if that is alright."

"I guess I can hold off leaving for a little bit," Zelig responded, "but make it quick. You don't want to keep my father waiting."

As Tanzi slowly placed the herbal tea in a container, she glanced out the window above her sink and caught a glimpse of a familiar face. Oren was outside. Silently, she shook her head indicating this was not a good time for him to come in for a visit.

Sensing her nervousness, Oren slipped around to one of the other windows to see who it was making her feel so uncomfortable. Once he caught sight of the young man freely rummaging through her papers and belongings, he knew immediately this visitor was trouble. Thinking back to Eber's cleverness in offering Mendi "special tea," causing him to sleep, he almost wished he could do the same for this young man. Unfortunately, he did not have any of that "special tea," so all he could do was watch as the stranger led Tanzi out her door and down the path.

Keeping a safe distance from Tanzi and the young man, he followed to see where she was being taken. After walking for a time, Oren recognized the region. They were heading towards Chana, a busy village with lots of activity.

With the light directing him as he went, he noticed it led him off the regular path towards a cabin sitting on the outskirts of the village. Though he was reluctant to lose sight of Tanzi, he chose to follow the light before him instead. The light stopped at an unfamiliar cabin. Oren cautiously stepped up to the window to look inside.

As he watched, a young girl moved around the room bringing tea and refreshments to an elderly woman sitting in a chair. Taking a closer look at the woman, he noticed she looked vaguely familiar. Deciding to take a chance, Oren approached the back door and knocked.

The young girl answered.

"Hi," he said, a little unsure on how to start his conversation. "I was walking through the woods and was directed to your house, but I'm not entirely sure why."

"You were directed here?" she asked. "How were you directed?"

"Well, a light led me here. A friend of mine was brought here by a young man and I was trying to find out what was going on. May I come in so I can explain myself better?"

From the other side of the house, Ms. Bina called over to Yona telling her to allow the man in.

"Well, Ms. Bina says you can come in," she replied while stepping aside for Oren to enter.

As he came inside, he had to ask, "Did you say her name is Ms. Bina?"

"Yes. This is Ms. Bina's cabin."

Oren immediately started laughing. "I know who you are!" he announced. "You are Jessah's friend and Ms. Bina is Miss Haddie's sister! I am good friends with both of them."

Yona was immediately set at ease while Oren walked across the room to greet the woman he had heard so much about.

"My name is Oren," he said as they shook hands. "I actually live some of the time in Miss Haddie's guest cottage," he explained, "and I see Jessah quite often. She is an amazing young lady, for sure!"

As they shook hands, Ms. Bina saw enough to realize that this man was indeed telling the truth. "Welcome Oren! You are my first guest since we began our battle against the plan of the village elders here."

"Well, thank you for allowing me to join you. I am always against any plans of the village elders! They have quite a reputation of control and destruction here on Kumani. Maybe I was sent here so I might be able to assist you," Oren speculated. "Why don't you tell me what is happening here in Chana."

As Oren sat down across from Ms. Bina, she described Yona's terrible circumstances with Zelig's selfish desires for the twelve-year-old to be his wife. In their conversation, Oren learned that Zelig's father, Cobar was actually one of the village elders who used his power and position to cater to his son's wishes. He soon figured out that the young man leading Tanzi to Chana was actually Zelig.

While considering all this new information, Ms. Bina mentioned that she had been visited recently by her sister and was given important wisdom on how to respond to this unethical plan. Yona, excited by the discussion, spoke up.

"We're planning a tea party!"

"A tea party?" Puzzled by this explanation, Oren wasn't sure how to respond. This was an area he was completely unfamiliar with. As he waited for a moment, listening to the one who had all the answers, it suddenly dawned on him—he might actually be able to help in an indirect manner.

Chapter Nine

CHEN'S INSTRUCTIONS

A clear trumpet blast echoed throughout the Eagles' Nest alerting all the residents that Chen had called a special meeting that morning. Most were already up preparing for the day. This sound indicated that they needed to hurry to arrive at the Hub. Though infrequent, trumpet blasts meant something important was to be announced.

Galen and Shoshanna were among the first to arrive at the Hub, standing wide-eyed as the residents poured in through the front doors to join the crowd gathering in the massive lobby. Shortly Roany and Uri also appeared and joined their friends as the people around them chatted excitedly.

"Have you heard what this is all about yet?" Roany asked Galen.

"Not yet, but I imagine we will all find out very shortly."

"I do hope this meeting starts soon," Uri agreed. "I haven't had breakfast yet and I'm hungry."

"Uri, I'm sure you'll have a chance to eat breakfast afterwards," Shoshanna encouraged him. "It probably won't last that long."

"Good! Cause when I get hungry, I can get a little impatient," he warned his friends.

Roany spoke up at that point. "Uri, none of us have had breakfast yet. I think we can eat a little later than normal."

"I can try," Uri responded, "but I'm not promising anything."

"I am sure you will be just fine," Galen assured him.

As they were talking, a familiar face passed by, causing the four friends to stop and gaze as he moved through the crowd. Without a word being said, a hush came over the crowd as the lone man walked up to the platform before them. All eyes were on him as he turned to face the group.

"Welcome, my friends," Chen began. "I am so glad you were all able to come this morning." His eyes scanned the assembly before him and though there were hundreds of people present, each felt a personal connection with him. Chen continued.

"We do have some new residents here at the Eagles' Nest and I would like to encourage each of you to let them know how happy we are they have joined us." Speaking to Galen, Shoshanna, Roany, and Uri, Chen asked if they would wave their hands so all the residents could see who they were. The crowd applauded their new neighbors briefly before Chen continued.

"Now, regarding the purpose of this gathering, I must first inform you that we have before us a great battle here in Kumani. This is not a war waged with chains, arrows, and axes, but a battle based on love, compelled by compassion, and freed by forgiveness."

The crowd cheered in agreement as Chen proceeded.

"As a people familiar with the ways of the eagle, we each carry within us the ability to see the residents of the lowlands free from the oppressive fear-based control held over them. Each of you has been invited to join us in this battle for their freedom. I am asking you to return first to your own villages below, two by two. Your people need you to speak the truth in love to those held captive by the lies they have been taught."

"Some people will receive this truth in joy. Others, unsure about what you are sharing, will listen and consider what you are saying. Later, they will respond. There will be those, however, who will completely reject all you have to say, either because of fear or their love of control. With these various responses, some of you will return here joyful with reports of those responding immediately. Others may not see the results of their encounters, but are victorious nonetheless."

Heads nodded as the people of the Eagles' Nest agreed with what Chen had to say.

"However, as you travel back to your home villages, some of you may also encounter those who will come against you. As a result, some will be cast into prison, while others may not return to us at all, but instead will begin their residence in their new eternal home with Elemet. Regardless of how the people respond, we must let them know there is another way for them to live. The clouds of darkness have dominated the villages of this island far too long! Now is the time for the people of the Eagles' Nest to rise up and take a stand for both truth and freedom!"

The people cheered loudly, applauding Chen's announcement. While they cheered, Galen, Shoshanna, Roany, and Uri looked at each other, unsure of how they felt about returning so soon to the family and friends they had just left behind. Chen proceeded.

"The ones who have been through all the training and needed preparations will be the first ones to be sent out," he explained. "Some of you will walk to your villages, some will be flown to their destinations, while others will be moved to their assigned locations. To hear the details of where and when each of you will be sent, I encourage you to check with Aquila at the assignment center. I am so honored to work with each of you as the light of truth is poured out upon our beloved Kumani! Thank you all!"

Again, the crowd responded in cheers as Chen stepped down and headed through the throng to exit. Uri, a bit confused about his assignment, pushed his way through the residents so he could speak with Chen directly. Before he'd gone too far, Chen was standing directly in front of him.

"Uri," Chen said. "You have a question for me?" A little stunned at his quick appearance, Uri needed a second to pull his thoughts together.

"Well, yes. I do have a question," Uri replied. "As you know, I really have no memory of where my home village is. My earliest recollections only go back to Camp Shabelle where I was trained."

"Yes. Camp Shabelle is the only home you have known," Chen agreed.

"So when I am sent out, where am I to go?"

With a smile of understanding, Chen answered, "You will go to your home, Camp Shabelle."

"Camp Shabelle? And what can I do there?"

"Are there not children there who need to hear the truth?" Chen responded. "Are there not jobs and positions which need to be filled?" Puzzled, Uri stared at Chen unsure of how to respond. Chen continued.

"With your unique background and upbringing, you are the perfect one to work your way into that place so you can speak to and encourage the children who are there," he explained. "First, you and your friends will finish your training here and then you will be sent out."

"Won't I be recognized as one of the escaped dissenters?" Uri asked.

"When the time comes, your appearance will be altered so you will not be recognized," Chen assured him. "There is a great need for additional staff at Camp Shabelle, so I am sending you. There is already one who has begun to teach the children truth, but your presence there will help maintain the spreading of truth and freedom among those young ones."

"And how long will I be there?" Uri questioned him.

"That is something that you will find out after you arrive," Chen smiled. "You know, you are the perfect man for that job!" Before Uri had a chance to respond, Chen moved on through the crowd and exited the Hub.

Uri, still stunned by what he had been told, stood silent as his three friends joined him.

"We saw you had a chance to speak to Chen," Shoshanna said as they arrived at Uri's side. "What did he have to say?"

"He said we would be completing our training before being sent out," Uri replied.

"That makes sense," Roany said. "I mean we only just arrived here yesterday."

"Did he tell you anything else?" Galen asked.

"Yeah. I told him I didn't really have a home village to return to. He said I would be going to Camp Shabelle."

"You mean Camp Shabelle, the orphanage?" Roany questioned him. "How is that going to happen? Only children are sent there."

"He said he was going to change my appearance so I wouldn't be recognized and that I was going to work there for a time," Uri responded. "I don't understand how all that is going to happen, but if Chen says so…"

"Of course, it will happen," Galen encouraged him. "Chen has a way of knowing things no one else does. Right?" The others all agreed heartily. "So, why don't we go see about some breakfast before we start our training?"

"That sounds good to me," Shoshanna replied.

As the four friends moved toward the galley for breakfast, Azriel watched them from a distance. His eye was upon one in particular, Shoshanna, but he couldn't help but notice the others in her party as well. There was something very different about the four newcomers that caught his attention. Though many before them had endured the passage through the smoking mountains, he could tell these novices were being groomed for a very special assignment on the island of Kumani. Only time would tell how both Chen and Elemet planned to use them.

Chapter Ten

A NEW DIRECTIVE

The bell rang as the door to the print shop was pushed open. With the memory of Yona's tears still planted firmly in his mind, Mendi took a breath as he entered. Seeing the great injustice being forced upon this young girl, he determined to make some changes on how he had lived his life until this point and this is where it needed to begin.

Stepping up to the counter, Mendi could see the man sitting at his desk was obviously engrossed in something, so he cleared his throat hoping to get his attention. Looking up briefly from the papers before him, the man was obviously irritated with this disruption.

"Can I help you with something?" the man asked gruffly, his eyebrows still furrowed in thought.

"Hi! I am looking for Cobar," Mendi said with a smile.

"I am Cobar. What can I do for you?"

"Well, actually I think the right question to ask is what can I do for you? Allow me to introduce myself. My name is Mendi and I am from the Kieran region. Since my younger years, I have been trained at Camp Shabelle as an infiltrator collecting personal information for those who need to know. Is this something that might interest you?"

Cobar, not impressed with his slick sales pitch, stood up from his desk and moved to the counter to better examine this young man. Looking him over for a moment, Cobar said.

"And why is it that you come to me offering your services?" he asked suspiciously. Mendi smiled brightly to cover the slight nervousness he felt.

"I was working with the village elders in my region and they suggested you might have need of my services here in Chana."

"You haven't mentioned why you left Kieran. How is it that the village elders there no longer need your services?" Cobar pressed him. He needed to know more about this young man before revealing anything.

"Well, I guess you could say my last assignment sort of 'burned up,'" Mendi replied, trying desperately not to disclose more than he wanted. He really needed this job.

"How was your assignment 'burned up?'" he asked. "That sounds a little odd."

"Yes, it definitely was a little odd," Mendi responded while attempting to recall all he had practiced saying on his journey to Chana. "All I know is that I was assigned to this older couple. I came over daily for a time, helping them out around their cabin while I got to know them better. Then, one day when I arrived at their house, they were gone and their cabin was completely burned down. Since my assignment obviously ended, I heard that you might still be hiring enforcers in this region. I decided to come and offer my skills to you."

"You say their cabin was burned down?" Cobar inquired. The mention of a fire relit his memory of his last village elders meeting where Hamah spoke of his plans to destroy the village of Yashen and all its inhabitants with fire while blaming it on the dissenters. "Was their cabin the only thing burned?"

"Yes. Only their cabin was burned down with nothing left behind."

A little relieved to hear that this fire was not the one Hamah spoke of, Cobar asked, "And you don't know how this happened?"

"No, I don't. I just discovered it that way."

Mendi was beginning to feel a little uncomfortable because he knew he was not disclosing everything about the incident. His throat grew dry as he waited for Cobar to continue.

Not wanting to mention the upcoming disaster, he simply responded, "That fire was most likely the work of dissenters in the area. So tell me exactly what you do as an infiltrator?"

"Well, I usually try to make friends with the people I am to report on. After making friends with them, I observe all their activities and learn all I can about them. Once they trust me, I report all that I find out to the village elders so they can respond appropriately."

"And you have been doing this for years, correct?"

"Yes, sir," Mendi responded.

Once again, Cobar grew silent for a time considering his options before reacting.

"Well, as an acting representative for the village elders in this region, I think I actually might have some people I may need you to befriend and then report back to me about."

"Oh, wonderful!" he responded in relief. Finally he had another job...and he promised Yona that he would get some information about her situation as well. "Where would you like to send me, sir?"

"I am concerned about one of the older ladies in our community," Cobar admitted. "She is blind and has one of our orphans helping her now. The orphan's name was added to our list of available young women recently and this woman became quite upset about it. She actually had the nerve to confront me about this decision! Can you imagine that?"

Mendi nodded sympathetically. "Terrible! And who is this woman?"

"Her name is Bina, Ms. Bina, and the orphan's name is Yona," he replied. "I think I might send you over there to 'help out' this old lady to make sure she isn't causing any trouble among our residents."

Once Yona's name was mentioned, Mendi's heart dropped. He knew this was going to put him in a difficult position as this was the very person he intended to help. Clearing his throat nervously, he worked to remain as calm and professional as possible.

"Not to question your decision in any way, but could I ask what threat a blind, old lady could possibly be to the operations of the village elders?"

"You are not already beginning to question my wisdom and influence with the village elders, are you?" Cobar retorted in anger.

"Oh, no sir! It's just that this Ms. Bina is blind. What could she possibly do?"

"If you do not want the job, I will be glad to find someone else to take your place! Either you do as I ask, or you can look elsewhere for work as an infiltrator. Is that clear?"

"Yes, sir! Perfectly clear!"

"Good! So I am giving you directions to her house. I expect you to befriend her, learn all you can about this woman, and then report back to me in a couple of days. Can you do that?"

"Oh, yes. That is not a problem!" Mendi forced a smiled as he quickly realized he was now in a very difficult position. He waited as Cobar wrote out the directions to the house he had just come from. He wondered how he was going to manage befriending Ms. Bina and reporting on her without betraying his new acquaintance, Yona.

Cobar tore off a piece of paper and handed it to Mendi. "As you are new to the village, we do have a small inn where you will be able to find a room to rent while you are here," he explained. "If I like the information you give me, the next time I see you, you will get paid. Is that clear?"

"Yes. Very clear, sir," Mendi replied after examining directions to Ms. Bina's house. "I will check back with you in a couple of days to let you know what I have learned about Ms. Bina. Thank you," he said as he exited the print shop with his heart beating hard. He had no idea what he was going to do!

Slowly Mendi moved down the road towards the inn Cobar had spoken of. At least he had a place to sleep for the night giving him a chance to figure out how he was going to take care of this problem.

Chapter Eleven

A TWIST IN THEIR PLANS

Several days had passed since Tanzi's forced visit with Cobar. Though she had nothing new to report to him, his gruff treatment and verbal threats had impacted her. With her dramatic change in loyalties, Tanzi worked hard to still appear committed to the village elders, but refused to speculate any further on what she had learned about Ms. Bina. Her lack of new information frustrated Cobar until she was finally dismissed.

By the time she arrived back home, her nerves were on edge. She knew Cobar's threats were very real. If she did not come up with something helpful to report soon, she knew she would end up in prison.

Cobar's increased intensity created some questions in her mind. *"What was the real motive behind his sudden hunger for more information? If Cobar was stirred up, the other village elders may be stirred up as well,"* she reasoned.

Known as an aggressive researcher and informant, Tanzi knew it was only a matter of time before the other village elders also called upon her to assist them.

Just as she was sitting in her kitchen trying to figure out her best options, someone knocked on her front door. Still jumpy from her surprise visit from Zelig, Tanzi quickly looked out her front window to see who it was before responding. Thankfully, she saw it was Oren.

Opening the door, she invited her friend in and quickly informed him of her forced visit to Chana and her meeting with Cobar. Oren could see she was upset, so he allowed her to unload all her worries and concerns about the situation.

"How much longer will I be able to cover my change of heart and desire to follow Elemet?" she asked.

"Well, the only way I know to counteract the plans of darkness is to fully respond to the light by following wherever it leads," Oren replied.

"What are you talking about?" Tanzi was confused by his answer. "I have responded to the light, but I don't know where the light is leading me. Do you?"

"The village elders have had easy access to you in your home. I may have a plan." Oren responded. "It may not be safer, but it certainly would be effective in dispelling darkness and spreading the light."

"You still haven't told me what this plan of yours is."

"This plan has actually come from Ms. Bina and I think you would be a marvelous asset, as long as we keep your identity hidden."

"And how are we going to do that?" she asked.

"Why don't we sit down so I can explain it to you?"

The two friends sat down in the living room as Oren described the plans he, Ms. Bina, and Yona had come up with. Tanzi listened astutely, learning how she could be a great resource in exposing the darkness.

Meanwhile, back at the Eagles' Nest, the couple being sent out on the first mission gave final hugs to friends and family. With no idea on how they would be received in their home village, they only knew it was time for them to share the ways of the eagle with those they had left behind. Chen had made it very clear. Some would return and some may not. With knapsacks filled with camping supplies, the couple waved goodbye as they began their journey.

Galen, Shoshanna, Roany, and Uri watched the husband and wife as they bravely embarked on whatever lay before them. Tears ran down Shoshanna's cheeks. She knew firsthand how quickly things can change while following the light. One moment she was still living at home with her father, and the next moment she was off climbing up the smoking mountain with three friends she had only recently met.

Taking a glance around her, Shoshanna was very grateful for the relationships that had developed during their journey. All the many challenges and experiences had only deepened her love for Elemet, Chen, and the ways of the eagle, but had also built a bond of appreciation for the three men now standing beside her.

Roany had grown to be a friend who was unafraid to question the motives behind decisions that were made. Uri, with his great size and strength was the one to notice the most obvious of things and yet had the gift of compassion for others in need.

And then there was Galen.

His encouragement along the way showed him to be a man of wisdom and a natural leader with a touch of humor mixed in to keep things light. Yes, he was someone she deeply admired. As she studied his black wavy hair and distinct brown eyes, she suddenly remembered his expressed desire to get to know her better once they arrived at the Eagles' Nest.

Just prior to their entry into the canyon, she recalled how she wanted to first enjoy her freedom as a single young woman before committing to any man. Azriel had noticed her and offered to train her to ride on the backs of the eagles. Exciting as that was to have such a handsome and strong warrior take notice of her, Shoshanna couldn't help but acknowledge her attraction to Galen.

Noticing Shoshanna's stares, Galen turned his head towards her with a smile. Blushing, Shoshanna quickly diverted her gaze elsewhere. As the crowd began to disperse, Galen boldly took hold of Shoshanna's hand while encouraging his other friends to return to the Hub so they could continue their training. At first, Shoshanna was embarrassed but soon grew accustomed to his hand assisting her along the way.

Both Uri and Roany noticed the hand-holding right away. Smiling at each other, they pressed through the crowd. Both anticipated the day would come when Galen would finally stake his claim on Shoshanna.

Another set of eyes also took notice of the couple holding hands on their way back to the Hub. Azriel watched from a distance. Though greatly impressed with Shoshanna and her inner strength, he knew that she and Galen had experienced much together on their journey to the Eagles' Nest. That was not something he could change, however, he did promise to teach her how to maneuver the golden eagles while flying on their backs. He was not quite ready to give up on winning Shoshanna's attention.

Chapter Twelve

A WALK IN THE GARDEN

The sun shone through the window in Jessah's room gently awakening her from a deep sleep. Slowly opening her eyes, she stretched as her world came into focus. Pressing her face against the window, she looked out at the surrounding gardens. Fruit trees of every variety filled the homestead with luscious fruit dangling from the branches. Vines groaned under the weight of the enormous grape clusters. Everything was so perfect here, and yet she wondered what had changed in the forest around them since she had last explored the region.

She clearly recalled Miss Haddie's instructions not to leave the safety of her homestead. As she reflected on her past adventures and exploits through the forest, pangs of longing hit her. She missed the freedom she once had to trek through the woods, climb vines, paddle canoes, and deliver messages to those walking in the ways of the eagle.

She yearned for new adventures!

Now, here she lay in a beautiful gilded cage where she was only allowed to roam the grounds and then briefly visit

Camp Shabelle several times a week. Her heart ached for some of the old ways.

As she lay in bed considering her situation, Jessah heard a familiar voice calling her.

"Jessah! Come walk with me in the garden," the voice said.

Without hesitation, Jessah was up and dressed. She ran out the door of the cottage with her eyes scanning the homestead gardens for the one she heard. After studying the grounds carefully, she was disappointed not to see anything out of the ordinary.

Thinking the voice was just a figment of her imagination, Jessah turned around to reenter the cottage. As she did, a brilliant light appeared before her forcing the girl to shield her eyes from its intensity.

"Jessah," he said with deep affection. "Look at me."

Slowly the girl's eyes adjusted to the form standing before her. The initial burst of light grew softer, allowing her to see the face of the one who called her. His white flowing robe hung loosely around him while rainbow-like prisms reflected light in every direction.

"Elemet!" she cried out. "It's you! I knew it had to be you!"

"Would you like to go for a walk with me in the garden?" he asked.

"Well, yes, but I have walked in this garden many times. I was actually hoping we might go somewhere else," Jessah admitted.

"Oh, I'm not talking about Miss Haddie's garden," he assured her. "I am referring to my garden, something you've never seen before."

"You have a garden?" she asked in wonder.

"Yes, I have a garden. In fact, I have many gardens—each different and unique."

"Oh, then I would love to see your garden! Where is it?"

Elemet smiled and stretched out his hand to the young girl. "Come and I will show you."

Eagerly, Jessah grabbed his hand and in an instant they were no longer walking on the familiar grounds of the homestead. Instead they were in a completely different location where nothing looked familiar at all!

"Where are we?" Jessah asked as she stared wide-eyed at flowers and vegetation she had never seen before. "This place is so beautiful, it can't be Kumani!"

"No, this is my personal garden," Elemet explained. "One that I designed for us to enjoy together. You may explore the garden for yourself if you like. You can't get lost here."

"Really?" she questioned him.

"Absolutely," he assured her. "As you explore, I will sit here on the bench waiting until you return. When you come back, I have some things to tell you."

Nodding, the girl strolled through the garden with her arms outstretched touching every flower, bush, and plant she could reach. Each felt so unique. Some felt so soft, she wanted to caress them for hours. Multi-hued flowers with tiny blossoms bundled together like a bouquet graced the bushes as she ran by.

There were rocks to climb, fields to run through, and enormous trees with iridescent butterflies and brightly colored birds flying all around her. Sweet fragrances filled the air as fluffy clouds passed through the blue skies overhead.

Finally, when Jessah felt as though every sense had been refreshed and stimulated, she walked back to the white bench where Elemet waited. Once there, she sat down and threw her arms around the one who made all things for her pleasure, hugging him.

"That was amazing!" she exclaimed, still out of breath from all her adventures in his garden.

"I am so glad you enjoyed it," Elemet responded. "I thought you might. So, are you ready to hear what I need to tell you?"

"Oh yes!" Jessah responded while laying her head upon his chest. "I am listening."

As Elemet spoke, Jessah listened intently as he explained some things that would shortly happen and what she was to do. After a time, Jessah found the soothing sound of his deep voice lulling her to sleep. She fought to keep her eyes open, but soon found it impossible.

Suddenly, Jessah opened her eyes and found she was back in her own bed. The sun was just arising, washing her room with light. Puzzled, the girl wondered if she just had a wonderful dream or was it a real encounter with Elemet like she had before. She had no idea.

Getting up from her bed, she dressed quickly and went out into the kitchen to investigate the incredible aromas filling the cabin. Miss Haddie was baking fresh muffins for breakfast! Excitedly, Jessah came out and immediately noticed the huge bouquet of flowers sitting on the table. She stared at the flowers in wordless wonder. Miss Haddie noticed her interest in the bouquet.

"Aren't they lovely?" she asked. "When I got up this morning, they were already sitting in a vase awaiting me. It must have been a gift from Elemet." Noticing that Jessah was still silent, Miss Haddie asked her if she was all right. Finally Jessah was able to respond.

"Oh, I am more than fine," she answered as she stared at the vibrant flowers, her eyes glistening with joy. Unlike anything growing on Miss Haddie's homestead, the blooms were a clear indication that her dream the night before had been a genuine encounter. With his deep voice still resonating in her mind, she was reminded to treasure the things she had been told, for they would certainly come to pass.

Chapter Thirteen

PLAN ACTIVATION

An eerie silence came from the village of Yashen as the dense smoke saturated the area. Carefully positioned fires had been set completely surrounding the quaint community. Special enforcers assigned to overseeing this task stood motionless, observing as cabin after cabin burned. Thick, black smoke streamed into the atmosphere above the silent village.

Though populated, the residents were no longer aware of the fires raging around their homes. All had been taken care of prior to the fires. Directions had been followed exactly by the drug-induced enforcers. In the end, only darkened eyes and clouded minds watched without emotion at the utter destruction of Yashen before them.

There were no survivors.

To prevent any disruption or intervention, enforcers had been stationed on every path or trail heading towards the village. Any travelers or hunters in the region were pointed in another direction. An explanation of fallen trees blocking the trails ahead were given to those asking the reason for the detour. Only when the job was done, would visitors be allowed into the vicinity. Carefully placed evidence would soon be positioned so all would think this was the work of the escaped dissenters.

With fear and terror stirred up afresh in the remaining lowlanders, village elders would have no trouble reestablishing their control over those under their domain. The islanders shortly would be convinced that submitting to their reign would be the only way to adequately protect them from the terrifying destruction of the dissenters.

Though the islanders would respond appropriately to this devious plan, Hamah actually had other purposes involved with his plot. The village elders would also submit to his bigger plan, leaving him alone as the one ultimately dictating the lives of everyone on Kumani. Backed up by the special enforcers he controlled, no one would dare challenge his rule.

Once viewed as a "crazy inventor," Hamah had worked many long years in the forgotten Camp Coshek experimenting and perfecting control over the dissenters sent there. Though first respected as only a contributor to the reign of the village elders, his plan from the beginning was to dominate all those he once worked with.

With Camp Coshek far from the other villages and with no one monitoring his work, Hamah slowly eliminated all his co-workers, replacing them with his drug-induced enforcers. Camp Coshek had become his domain and now the time had come for him to expand his rule to include the hapless village elders.

Though not present to watch the burning of Yashen, Hamah was close by. He had great confidence in his special enforcers' ability to finish the task exactly as prescribed. As he moved closer to the residence of the chief village elder, he had to smile at the perfection of his plan currently unfolding. The distinct increase of black smoke permeating the surrounding haze indicated his devious plan had been accomplished. The next step in his plan would soon be executed as he proceeded towards Chana. The chief village elder would be informed of the modifications he had put into place.

Meanwhile, up beyond the smoking mountains in the Eagles' Nest, wave after wave of gallant men and women made their own journeys down to the lowlands. A number of them had already departed and those awaiting their appointed time looked forward to their own return as well.

The Hub was busy with training and instructions for all the residents, however, up in a room overlooking the expanse of the Eagles' Nest, Chen stood looking out the window somberly as a knock sounded at his door.

"Come in, Azriel," he responded without moving. Azriel, poked his head in before entering.

"You sent for me?"

"Yes. I have some news for you," Chen replied. "Please come in." Sensing the seriousness of the moment, Azriel stepped in and joined Chen in looking over the vibrant basin before them. Respectfully, he waited until his friend and mentor was ready to speak. After a few moments of silence, Chen continued.

"It has begun."

"What do you mean?" Azriel questioned him.

"The village of Yashen has been completely burned down. There were no survivors," he added sadly. "With their poisoned waters and the toxic fires burning all around them, they had no chance to escape."

"I'm so sorry. It must be a traumatic thing for you to see."

"Yes, but I am relieved that Ilia and Akim were able to arrive there prior to the fire. They spoke with many of their friends urging them to call upon Elemet. With that warning, some of the residents managed to escape the deadly flames, but not all of them listened," Chen explained solemnly.

"And what of Ilia and Akim?"

"They stayed with those who remained," he replied as he gazed into Azriel's eyes. "You would have been proud of them. They encouraged the villagers and retained their joy and peace even until the end."

A single tear ran down Azriel's face as he recalled the young couple joyfully leaving the Eagles' Nest on their assignment. Placing his hand upon Azriel's shoulder, Chen encouraged him.

"They both knew when they left here that they would not be returning. My father, Elemet welcomed them all home with great joy."

Shaking his head in amazement, Azriel responded, "They knew and yet they were still so happy to return to Yashen."

"Yes, when you know the truth, suddenly time on Kumani appears very fleeting, especially when you discover the endless life found in Elemet."

Azriel swallowed hard before continuing. He and Akim had been close friends. Though he knew they were in a much better place, his heart still ached for their Eagle's Nest family still present. "How do you want me to address this?"

"You can let the residents of Eagles' Nest know that although our friends have perished, they live along with many of the people they spoke with prior to the fires," Chen responded. "Much rich seed has been deposited on this island and now it is time to reap the harvest."

"Yes, I will let the residents know, Azriel replied. "Am I still to head up those flying by eagles to the distant regions we spoke of?"

"Yes. The timing on this is very important. How close are you to completing their training?"

"My recruits are nearly ready. We have been successfully practicing maneuvers and landings on a regular basis."

"Good!" Chen was obviously pleased with his diligence. "Very soon I will be calling upon you and your trainees to execute the plan."

Azriel, encouraged by Chen's words, nodded and prepared to leave the room. Just as he opened the door to exit, Chen called out to him.

"You are a good man, Azriel! Both my father and I are proud of you."

Looking back at Chen's blazing blue eyes, Azriel felt a sudden impartation of love hit him which nearly knocked him off his feet. He hung onto the door to steady himself momentarily before responding.

"Thank you, Chen! That means so much to me."

"Go in peace. There is nothing to fear."

Nodding in response, Azriel headed out the door while attempting to keep his balance as he walked. He relished those moments with Chen as did the other residents of Eagles' Nest. However, the time had come to refocus on completing the training required for those he was to lead. Even as he walked down the hallway, he wondered if he too would be asked to lay down his life in this assignment or if he was returning afterwards. Whatever the outcome, Azriel was ready.

Chapter Fourteen

TAKING OVER

The front door of the print shop burst open as a dark figure entered. Startled by the force of entry and the bell announcing a visitor, Cobar looked up, annoyed by the disruption. Once he saw who had entered, his throat ran dry as he stood to greet Hamah. He was not expecting to see him in his place of business.

"Sir Hamah!" he greeted him trying to sound relaxed and cheerful. "What brings you to our village?"

"I have a message for you to deliver to all the village elders before our next gathering."

"Oh? And why am I the chosen person to deliver this messag?" Cobar asked. He had hoped the hooded garbs had hidden his identity at the gatherings, but Hamah was not fooled.

"You are the chief village elder, correct?"

Cobar cleared his throat and nervously glanced around before answering. He was not accustomed to sharing this information in public.

"What makes you think I am the chief village elder?" he asked weakly, attempting to maintain his cover.

"I have informants you are not yet aware of. I wouldn't suggest arguing with me," Hamah responded with growing intensity. Immediately, Cobar yielded to the dark force peering through Hamah's eyes.

"Okay, Hamah. Let's not get upset. I can certainly deliver whatever message you need to send out."

"Good. Why don't we find a private place to talk so you can write down everything I'm about to tell you?"

"Certainly. We can do that. Let me call my son in so he can take care of the office while we talk," Cobar responded uncomfortably. He was not looking forward to being alone with Hamah in the least, but what choice did he have? Opening the door behind him, Cobar called for Zelig. Once his son understood his instructions, Cobar reluctantly followed Hamah to a private booth with high backed walls in one of the nearby inns where they could talk.

Seated with cups of hot tea before them, Hamah dictated the message Cobar was to deliver.

"First, you will let all the village elders know that things have changed for all the residents of Kumani. The haze we have been creating for many years at Camp Coshek has been altered and we have treated all the fresh water sources on the island with new pollutants that will help make this transition period much easier for everyone."

Cobar stopped writing for a moment and looked hard at Hamah. He had to ask.

"Exactly what transitional period are you referring to?"

"I'm glad you asked," Hamah responded with a smile. "This is the time where I step in as ruler over all the island and you become my subjects."

"What are you talking about? Village elders have been overseeing the activities of this island for many generations. We don't need a ruler."

"Actually, you do. With the changes already made in the haze blowing over the island and the fresh waters infected with my concoctions, you will soon find that the herbs you are already taking will not be effective any longer. I alone have the antidote for both the haze and the poisoned waters throughout the island. The degree of effectiveness against these pollutants will depend entirely upon my level of confidence in those following my directives."

Cobar sat stunned as Hamah continued.

"For example, those currently operating as village elders will have a choice to either fully cooperate or die a slow painful death as the toxins saturate their bodies. I will distribute enough antidote for each elder and their families for only one week. At the end of the week, I will decide if they have successfully cooperated, or if I will need to cut their supplies off."

"And what of the villagers?" Cobar inquired.

"Well, I will decide their fates based upon the skills I find necessary. May I remind you that we live on an island and we will run out of space if we don't keep the population growth under control," Hamah replied. "I will send my enforcers to take a census of the villages and when we find the numbers are getting too high, I will eliminate the elderly, sick, or weak as needed."

"Just in case you are wondering, I have also decided that some villages will be destroyed just as we did with Yashen. I will relocate those deserving life to key villages so it will be easier to monitor and control them rather than having them spread all over the place. I am currently deciding which villages will remain and which ones will be destroyed."

With his heart pounding and eyes downcast, Cobar asked, "And what have you decided for the village of Chana?"

"I'm not sure yet. I'm still thinking about it," he said with a dark smirk. "So, have you got all the information straight? I'd like to see this message delivered immediately so we can have our first gathering under my leadership by next week. That's when I will administer the antidote to those complying with my demands. Understand?"

"Yes. Perfectly. And may I ask how long will it be before the effects of the toxins are felt?"

"Oh, I suspect you will notice increasing weakness with difficulty focusing within the next several days," Hamah replied. "I encourage you to hurry and get the word out to the other village elders before you become too feeble to care."

With his knees shaking, Cobar stood to his feet in shock. Numbly, he moved towards the door. Hamah called after him just before he exited.

"Oh, and you can call me 'Lord Hamah' from this point on. I'm sure I will be hearing from you soon."

As soon as Cobar left, Hamah finished his tea, paid his tab, and exited the inn. Once both men departed, Mendi stuck his head out from a booth behind the one the two men had sat in.

He heard everything.

With his own heart pounding, Mendi paid for his food and rushed back to his room in the inn. He wanted to make certain that no one, especially Cobar, saw him emerging from the building he and Hamah had just met in. Knowing the full details of what Hamah planned for the island of Kumani sent chills down his spine. The deviousness of the plot sickened him as he thought about the unsuspecting villagers who would soon discover that the only way to survive would be to submit to Hamah in every aspect of their lives.

Panic set in as he tried to think of what he could possibly do to help stop Hamah. He was only one man, new to Chana, with no one he could call upon for support. Twelve-year-old Yona and Cobar were the only two people he knew in the village, but then he remembered Ms. Bina. She was old. She was blind, but for some reason, Cobar was afraid of her. Maybe Ms. Bina would have some answers, or at least know where he could go to stir up some kind of resistance against this new plot.

Realizing they all had only days before the new drug-induced haze began affecting their ability to think, he decided that he to take his chances and contact Yona and Ms. Bina after nightfall. He didn't want anybody seeing him. This was far too important to take a chance on getting caught! While waiting in his room for nightfall, Mendi carefully wrote down everything he had heard that afternoon so he could accurately relay all the information to Ms. Bina and Yona later.

Chapter Fifteen

TEA TIME

Ladies and young girls throughout the village and even some from neighboring villages emerged upon the streets of Chana. Dressed up and excited to be together, they strolled in from every direction, all heading towards one cabin located on the outskirts of the village. Ms. Bina had sent word through several of her friends in town that she was planning a tea party, something that had not been done in quite a long time.

Though the invitation had been extended to the ladies and their daughters in Chana, somehow word had gotten out beyond the village boundaries. The sight of women coming out from cabins all around made many of the men quite nervous. They were not used to seeing so many of the womenfolk all together at the same time.

As they knocked to announce their arrival, Yona opened the door for each of the guests, one after another, until every seat was taken and still they came. At one point, Yona rushed over to Ms. Bina to let her know the chairs were all taken, but she insisted that every woman be allowed to attend her tea party even if they all had to stand.

Several of Ms. Bina's neighbors noticed that cups for the tea where running short, so they hurried to their own cabins to bring more cups for everyone to use. Excitement filled the cabin as the ladies happily chatted with both new and old friends. The young girls accompanying their mothers found a corner in which they were able to sit upon the floor and visit as well.

As Yona rushed around with the kettle filled with hot water and tea provided by Miss Haddie, she suddenly noticed that the cabin appeared much larger than she remembered. Had the room grown in size? This puzzled her, but she was too busy to think much about it.

Suddenly there was a knock on the back door where she and Jessah often met. Their expected guest of honor finally arrived. As she opened the door, her new friend, Oren, greeted her.

"Hi Yona! It sounds like things are quite busy here," he said with a smile.

"You have no idea! I have never seen so many ladies gathered together before. Ms. Bina certainly has a lot of friends!" Yona replied. "Did you bring our special guest?"

"Oh yes."

Stepping aside, Oren motioned for a dark hooded woman standing behind him to step forward. Impressed with the well-dressed lady before her, Yona quickly invited them both in hoping that no one had seen their entry. From what Oren had told them about her, her colorful history had left her with a reputation as an informant. Though things had changed drastically in her life, she had to use great wisdom each time she moved around.

Once in the kitchen, the woman drew back her hood and smiled at the preteen before her. With long, black glistening hair and her stunning dark eyes, Yona almost felt intimidated by her beauty. Holding out her hand in greeting, the woman spoke.

"Hello Yona," she said. "I am Tanzi. I have heard so much about you and your friend, Jessah. Oren here has told me all about you and how brave you have been. It is so wonderful to finally meet you in person," she said as they shook hands.

"I am so honored that you were willing to come to our tea party. Ms. Bina asked me to let her know when you arrived so we can begin our meeting. Can I get either of you anything before I speak to Ms. Bina?" Yona asked.

"Maybe just a cup of tea would be nice," Tanzi answered.

"How about you, Oren? Would you like some tea?" Yona checked.

"Yes, tea sounds wonderful, especially if it is Miss Haddie's tea!" he replied.

"It is definitely Miss Haddie's tea," she said with a smile. "On her last visit, Miss Haddie brought us a huge supply. I guess she knew there would be a lot of people attending our tea party. I'll get your cup and then let Ms. Bina know we are ready."

Yona quickly put some tea into the cups, poured the hot water, and handed them to their newest guests before slipping out into the living room. As the door opened, Oren was surprised to see how many ladies were in attendance and how large Ms. Bina's simple living room now appeared.

"Wow!" he commented. "There are a lot of ladies out there!"

"Does that intimidate you some?" Tanzi asked with a smile.

"Maybe a little," he admitted. "When I was working as a butcher in my village, I did have quite a few ladies coming in to make their purchases, but they only came in a few at a time. That is a lot of femininity out there! Glad I don't have to go in with you."

"I would enjoy seeing you surrounded by so many ladies," Tanzi teased. "I think it's good for a man to feel outnumbered every once in a while."

"Maybe so, but not today. With all this new information about village elders coming out, a man might find himself taken down and tied up if he stuck his head out there! I think it might be safer for me to just listen from the kitchen, thank you very much!"

Recalling their earlier discussion, Oren continued, "So, you are going to keep your identity hidden when you go in there?" Tanzi hesitated a moment before replying.

"I don't know," she confessed. "Somehow I feel as though these ladies need to know who I am so they can trust what I share with them."

"It is your decision," Oren counseled her, "but understand that if your identity is revealed and even one lady

91

shares what she has heard with one of the village elders, you could be in great danger."

Looking downward for a moment, Tanzi agreed. "I realize that, but after all the trouble I have caused you and others in my past, I feel Elemet may be calling me to be completely transparent with these ladies, regardless of what happens to me."

"Well, if you are going to do that, I am going to do everything I can to protect you."

"Thank you, Oren, but that is not necessary."

"It may not be necessary, but I feel compelled to try anyway," he responded. "We can talk more about this after the tea party when I escort you home."

"Agreed."

Just as the two friends finished their discussion, Yona swung open the door with instructions from Ms. Bina.

"Ms. Bina says for you to take a seat in the back of the room and wait until she has finished all she is planning on sharing with the ladies. She says you will know when it is time to speak up."

"I am ready," Tanzi replied. "Show me where you want me to sit."

Nodding, Yona led Tanzi into the living room as Oren watched. His mouth grew dry as he thought about the risk and boldness it took Tanzi to publicly speak out in the very village where she had been questioned and threatened by Cobar only days before. Already thinking ahead, Oren decided he and Tanzi would need to make a quick exit shortly after she spoke.

He didn't know if any village elders or enforcers had noticed the huge influx of women pouring into Ms. Bina's home. Though things seemed to be unusually quiet outside when he arrived, he couldn't be certain that all the chatter coming from the other room was not filtering into Chana, alerting the men of this gathering. If necessary, he would find a way to include Tanzi in stepping with him into his "safe zone" should any investigators come across their path.

He took another sip of tea just as he heard Ms. Bina call their "tea party" to order.

With Yona now sitting at her side, Ms. Bina welcomed all the visitors to her home and made sure everyone had been served tea. They had, so Ms. Bina started by explaining the real purpose of their gathering that afternoon. With clarity and passion, the woman described the situation they found themselves in once Yona discovered her name on the list of available young women.

"For many generations we have watched our young men be assigned jobs and apprenticeship positions and have seen our young women assigned as wives to whomever the village elders chose. We've been told that these things must be done in order to safeguard our survival and future on the island of Kumani." The ladies all nodded as they listened intently. Ms. Bina continued.

"I, myself, submitted to the directives of the village elders when I was young, just as all of you have as well. Unfortunately, when it came to Yona, the young orphan assigned to me as a helper, I objected to her name being added to the list. You see, she is only twelve years old."

Several of the ladies gasped in surprise. One lady called out from the group, "Did you let them know she was only twelve?"

"Oh yes. However, I was informed that the village elders had deemed her prepared for marriage. Once they made their decision, I was told I could not challenge them without being labeled a dissenter."

"Couldn't you speak to one of the village elders about this?" another lady asked.

"Actually, I learned I *was* speaking with a village elder and it was his son who wanted Yona as his wife regardless of how young she is."

Angry chatter broke out among the ladies as they discussed this case among themselves.

"And what of my eleven-year-old Letitia? Is some village elder's son going to demand her for a wife as well?" another woman called out angrily. "That's not what all this was supposed to be about! Are they going to start telling us who can have children and which of our children will be permitted to live? Are they also going to decide how long the elderly can exist or will they put limits on that as well? This is too much!"

"Well, actually they have already been doing many things without our knowledge," one woman spoke up.

"And how do you know that?" someone challenged her.

Rising up, Tanzi stood before all the women. For a moment she scanned all their eyes which were filled with worry and concern over the growing injustices and control they could now see. She could remain unidentified and just speak her peace, but so many things had already been hidden from these dear people. It was time for her to lay everything out so they could fully comprehend the plots and schemes they were all victims of.

"My name is Tanzi," she began. "Not that long ago, I too had been convinced that the wisdom of the village elders was the only way to live and thrive on Kumani. Their lies became a part of me. So thorough was my indoctrination that I began working with them. I attended their meetings, I encouraged their decisions, and assisted in gathering information for them. I even reported my own son's best friend as a dissenter and helped with his arrest."

Again the room grew silent as they listened to the woman's voice behind them. Boldly, Tanzi walked up to the front and stood next to Ms. Bina's seat.

"I am not proud of what I did. I hurt a great number of people in my pursuit of excellence and success. Fortunately, I was stopped before things got any worse. Now I see how deceived and blind I was. I learned of another way to live. A way where I do not have to be in bondage to fear, but can be free to live in an uncommon manner."

"So are you saying that we have been deceived our whole lives?" another woman asked.

"If you are anything like me, I would say we have been taught many things that are not true. We have embraced these lies and have allowed fear to keep us in check. I believe it is time for you to hear the truth so you can decide for yourselves how you want to live."

"And what is this truth you speak of?" someone questioned her.

"I'm glad you asked," Tanzi replied.

The entire room full of ladies and young girls sat mesmerized as Tanzi described her own blindness and then her encounter with Chen when he explained the truth to her.

Chapter Sixteen

THE SEND OFF

Azriel had positioned himself out of view, but in a location where he could catch Shoshanna before she entered the lodge where she was staying. It wasn't too long before she appeared escorted as always, by her three companions. They said their goodnights and left. Azriel jumped down from his hidden perch and suddenly appeared in front of the young woman.

"Azriel! You startled me," Shoshanna exclaimed. "What are you doing?"

"With those three friends of yours always hanging around, I figured this would be the only way I could catch you alone," he explained. "It's so beautiful here at night, I thought you might enjoy seeing some of my favorite views before you went to bed. It won't take much time. You interested?" he asked. His boyish enthusiasm and excitement made it hard for Shoshanna to turn down.

"Okay," she agreed, "but promise me we won't be back too late. I am pretty tired and we have our last day of training before we meet with Chen."

"I promise. However, as far as training to fly on the eagles, that may have to be delayed. Chen has informed me that our group will be flying out in the next several days, I believe," Azriel explained. "Maybe when I return, we can go flying. Is that all right?"

"Of course. So exactly where are you taking me now?"

"Just follow me and you will see."

Curious to see what Azriel was so excited about, Shoshanna walked beside him, listening as he discussed all the new moves he and his team had been practicing that week.

"You see, when you press your body against the eagle's body you become as one," he said. "When you feel the eagle turn, you turn with him.

When it's time to land, you press your legs against him a little harder as he swoops down to the ground."

"Sounds amazing!"

"It is exhilarating!" he admitted as he ran ahead, leading the way to a quaint stone bridge before them. In the center of the bridge he stopped facing out toward the horizon. Shoshanna caught up and joined him looking out at the thousands of twinkling candles burning in the windows of each cottage that lay below. Beyond that, the shores of Kumani could be seen in the distance with the endless blue ocean reflecting the orange, reds, and yellows of the setting sun.

Looking upward, she noticed the brilliant sea of stars sparkling above them. Though she had seen the night skies for the first time while ascending the smoking mountains, the stars still took her breath away. Still looking up, she felt his hand slip over her own and give it a squeeze. Drawing back, Shoshanna looked at Azriel questioningly.

"Did I offend you?" he asked.

"No. I don't know what's happening. Something just doesn't feel right," Shoshanna replied.

"I have noticed you and Galen seem very close."

"Yes, it's true. We have been through a lot together before arriving here and I feel like I need to give that relationship some time for it to develop. Enjoying you as a friend is important to me, but loyalty to Galen is my first priority right now," Shoshanna explained. "Do you understand?"

"I do. It seems both Galen and I have seen the same inner beauty in you that we find attractive," Azriel admitted, but quickly said, "Not to say your outer beauty is not as appealing as well!"

"Well, thank you!" Shoshanna laughingly replied. "I'm so glad you understand."

After a few more moments of enjoying the view, Azriel respectfully suggested he escort her back to the lodge. Shoshanna agreed, so the two walked back slowly as the light waned.

"Thank you so much for showing me this view. It is absolutely lovely."

"And thank you for being honest with me. I just needed to find out how serious you were about Galen. And when I get back, you don't have to go flying with me if that would make Galen uncomfortable," Azriel added. "If I was courting you, the idea of you flying with another man would be rather unsettling."

"Yes, it might bother Galen. Thank you for being sensitive about that."

"We can still be friends though," Shoshanna reminded him. "I'm sure there are many things about the Eagles' Nest that we have not yet discovered. It would be fun to have you show us around sometime."

"Yes, that would be fun," he admitted. "Once we all get back from our missions, we can plan that."

"Wonderful!" Once they returned to the lodge, Shoshanna extended her hand to say good night. Azriel grabbed her hand and kissed the top of it respectfully.

"You truly are an amazing woman. I honor you as a daughter of Elemet. Thank you for spending this time with me!"

"Thank you, Azriel. And may your mission flying with the eagles be successful."

"Thank you. Good night, Shoshanna."

"Good night." Shoshanna turned and entered the lodge knowing she had made the right decision.

Azriel walked away that night in peace, realizing Elemet's plans and ways were so much better than anything he could ever figure out. Now that he knew where Shoshanna stood, he was free to focus solely on the mission before him.

The following morning, the three young men met Shoshanna as usual. They waked together towards the Hub to complete the last of their training sessions before finding out where and when they would be sent out. Uri knew he was to be sent to Camp Shabelle, but Roany, Shoshanna, and Galen wondered about the details of their own assignments. Uri was told his identity would be hidden, but what about them? With bounties placed on their heads and drawings of them circulated all over the lowlands, they might have some difficulties returning to their own villages. Roany had some ideas on the subject.

"What if we traveled with hoods over our faces and only spoke with people at night when they couldn't see who we are?" he suggested.

"I don't think I would speak to someone who wears a hood and only wants to speak with me at night," Shoshanna responded laughing. "That's too much like what the village elders do."

"That's true," Roany admitted with a smile. "I don't think I would speak to me either."

"Maybe all of us will have our identities hidden," Uri suggested.

"Speaking of that, I wonder if we saw Uri while he was under cover, would we still recognize him?" Roany mused.

"Oh, I wouldn't worry about that," Galen chimed in. "Take a good look at his size. How many men do you know that are that big?" Roany took another look at Uri and had to agree. He was definitely one of a kind!

Laughing, the foursome finally arrived at the Hub, anxious to finish their training. Daily they were seeing more and more of the residents heading out on their own assignments. Though they loved the Eagles' Nest, they wanted to do their part to reach their friends and family members still bound by the lies and fears which had enslaved at one time.

Before entering the room, they were stopped by a familiar face. Chen stood before them and requested that they join him for a time. Without hesitation, all four followed the man they had grown to love.

Chen led them into a small room so they could speak privately. Once they were seated, Chen began by encouraging them all for the quick progress they had made in their training.

"Your progress and preparation has brought both my father and me great joy. We've been watching you closely and are proud as we observe the choices you have made since you've arrived. This has demonstrated to us that you are ready to be released into the next portion of your gifting—setting captives free."

The four friends exchanged glances as each of them recalled moments when they had to choose between what might have been easy and then the better way. Shoshanna, in particular, was uncomfortable realizing that Chen was aware of her encounter with Azriel the night before. The three men appeared equally uncomfortable as they were each thinking of choices they had made in their recent past. Thankfully, Chen did not bring up personal examples, but simply proceeded with the purpose of his meeting with them.

"As you know, all four of you have been identified by what the village elders call 'the escaped dissenters.' Extra enforcers have been hired to look for you specifically. To the elders, you have become a threat to their control over the villagers, but to the people, you have become heroes. For this reason, Elemet and I have decided that at the proper time Uri will be assigned to encourage and help the children of Camp Shabelle. As for you three, we are sending you to help those fleeing the plotting village elders. You will be working with Oren, the woodsman, directing and leading the people to a place of safety."

Shoshanna's mouth dropped open when Chen said she would be working with her father. It had been quite a long time since she last saw him. Bursting inside, she contained her excitement allowing Chen to continue his instructions.

"With your assistance, the refugees will arrive at the homestead of Eber and Giza where they will receive necessary provisions and instruction."

At the mention of his parents, Galen's face lit up. He was thrilled at the idea of seeing his own parents again! But noticing that Roany's mother, Tanzi, had not been mentioned, Galen was almost tempted to ask Chen, but decided to hold his tongue until he was finished with his instructions. Chen proceeded.

"This is a very challenging time for all lowlanders. There are a great number of devious developments in play at this time that will require you and all those you are working with to listen very carefully to the instructions of my father and follow the light exactly as it directs you. Any deviation may result in either death or torment from those captive to the darkness."

"When you return, you will hear a great many tales of destruction, loss, and imprisonment, but don't let the works of darkness overcome you. There is another force at work in you that will eliminate the effects of both the haze and the tainted waters. A new ruler has recently emerged and through terror, he is causing even the village elders to bow to his authority. Fear has no place in your hearts and minds. Only confidence in the one who loves you will lead you as you lead others to freedom. The freedom I speak of is not just physical freedom, but the truth that allows freedom within. That can never be taken away."

"You will learn a great many more details when you arrive back in the lowlands. Some of it may shock you, but none of it can affect you if you will hold closely to the ways of the eagle. Look at things from a higher perspective and don't allow current circumstances to change what you know is true. Elemet and I are always with you."

"Now, let me explain exactly how you will be moving around Kumani," Chen stated. For the next hour, all four friends heard things they had never heard before and learned of ways far beyond anything they had ever experienced.

When Chen was done, they stood to exit the room, nearly numb from all the things that had been shared with them. But, before Roany left the room, Chen stopped him.

"Roany, I want to let you know that your mother will also be a part of this battle of truth. She has already taken the first step in speaking out against the lies of the elders at great personal risk. There will be a point when you will see her again as well. Stand strong, my friend, for a great number of lives will be impacted by her and those she is now working with."

With tears forming in his eyes, Roany thanked Chen for his kindness in sharing this information. As he left the room, he had to thank Elemet as well for allowing both him and his mother to be a part of this assignment. Soberly, he joined his friends as they headed out of the Hub with Chen's words still ringing in their ears.

Though they didn't fully understand everything Chen was referring to yet, they knew that once they returned to the lowlands, the questions they had would certainly become clear.

Chapter Seventeen

PROTECTED

"So you are saying that Ms. Bina's cabin was not that big before the tea party?" Tanzi asked.

"No. In fact, I would describe it as an average-sized cabin," Oren responded.

"Yes, everything about that meeting was extraordinary. Did I tell you that some of the women want to plan their own tea parties as well and would like me to come?"

"No, you didn't tell me. Are you sure you want to continue doing this? With all the extra enforcers roaming the forests, traveling could be risky," Oren warned her.

"In the past, I put quite a few people in danger," she reminded him. "Elemet has done so much for me. I feel that if I can help even one person to recognize the lies they have submitted to, it will be worth it."

"That sounds very noble of you, but remember that taking undue risks just to try and 'pay back' Elemet for what he has done is not what he wants either," Oren explained. "All Elemet has done for us is a gift. We can't earn a gift. Neither should we try to pay him back for that gift. A gift is freely given. Our job is simply to receive what he has given and then freely follow wherever he leads us so others can receive his gift as well."

As hard as that concept was to understand, Tanzi finally accepted the fact that she could never do enough to fully pay back Elemet for all he had done. The best one could do on Kumani was to fully surrender everything, allowing Elemet and his light to direct. Even as Oren was explaining this, he suddenly noticed that the light before him indicated it was time to hide behind one of the trees.

With Tanzi's cabin close by, he pulled his friend behind the tree, signaling her to be quiet as he slowly approached her home. When he drew closer, he saw several young men fleeing, leaving the doors wide open as they left. Once he confirmed that the intruders were gone, he called for Tanzi to join him at her front door.

Standing beside him, Tanzi's mouth dropped open as she surveyed the damage. Every storage area in her cabin had been opened with its contents strewn across the floor. Broken shards of pottery from what remained of her dishes were scattered everywhere. As they examined the other rooms, they found that nothing remained untouched.

"This was obviously the work of Cobar and his enforcers," Oren surmised. "Somehow I don't think he believed you when you said you had no more information to share with him. And with all this mess, you would have no way of knowing if they found anything important."

"Well, I am sure they didn't get anything that might be useful in their search for the dissenters," she replied.

"How do you know that?"

Taking off the knapsack she carried with her, Tanzi reached in and produced an old rolled up parchment.

"And what is that?" he asked.

"This contains some of Roany's notes. In it there are some references to Miss Haddie, the Eagles' Nest, and a few other important details that maybe you could help me figure out."

"I thought you already shared all that information at the village elders' meeting you attended."

"Well, let's just say I shared some of what I knew. There actually were some other important details that I withheld just because they were treating me so poorly...and I didn't fully understand them myself," she laughed.

"And how is it that you happened to be carrying this document with you?"

"Well, after meeting Chen, I knew I had to keep this information safe, so I bring it with me whenever I leave my cabin," she explained. "Also, just having something belonging to Roany brings me a little comfort. I do miss my son."

"I totally understand," Oren replied. "I miss my daughter as well." The two stood silent for a moment as they looked around. "Well, there doesn't appear to be much here for you to salvage, that's for sure. With this new attack, I don't think it is a good idea for you to stay in your home any longer."

"But, where will I go?" she asked.

"I know of a place where I'm sure you can be a great help and be spared attacks like this in the future."
"And where is that?" she asked puzzled.

"Why don't you first see if there is anything you would like to salvage from this mess and then I can tell you about this place. So, do you have a cart we can use for our journey?"

"Oh yes. You'll find it behind my shed."

"Great!" Oren responded as he headed towards the back.

Tanzi walked through the rooms of her cabin looking for anything that might be useful for their trip while Oren found the old cart she spoke of. After making a few minor repairs, the cart was ready to go. As he pulled it around to the front of her house, he found Tanzi waiting with some clothing, a few pots, and some food she found untouched.

While loading up the cart, Oren wondered if he should mention what was on his mind, or just let it go. He decided to say nothing, allowing Elemet to speak to her directly. Just as they finished packing, Tanzi stepped inside her home for one final item. When she returned, she had a burning candle in her hand.

"What is that for?" Oren asked.

"Well, your home was burned down when you left," she explained. "Maybe my home should be burned down as well. That way Cobar and the enforcers will not be able to use it for their own purposes. Right?"

"That's probably true," Oren responded. "I actually was thinking the same thing, but what is the candle for?"

"I have already started a fire on the inside of the cabin and thought maybe you could start it from the outside as well. Weren't we just talking about fully surrendering everything to Elemet? With my cabin gone, it will feel like my old life is gone as well. Would you like to start the fire for me?" she asked with a smile.

"Gladly!" Oren responded. It didn't take him long to set up kindling and logs next to the home. Once the cabin was fully engulfed in flames, they turned and began their trek towards Tanzi's new beginning.

Chapter Eighteen

A LATE NIGHT VISITOR

The last of the tea cups were just being washed when Yona and Ms. Bina heard a loud knocking on their back door.

"Goodness gracious!" Ms. Bina commented. "Who would be coming to see us at this hour?"

"Maybe one of the ladies forgot something," Yona suggested. "I'll see who it is." Tired from all the clean-up after their tea party, Yona took the time to dry her hands before going to the door. Just before she answered, their visitor knocked again.

"I'm coming!" she called out before opening the door.

As soon as the door cracked open, their visitor pushed his way in and quickly shut the door behind him, breathing hard.

"Mendi!" Yona exclaimed. "What are you doing here?"

"I'm so sorry. I just had to make sure I wasn't being followed," he explained as he rushed past her to peek out the front window.

"Yona, who is our guest? I don't recognize his voice," Ms. Bina asked.

"I'm sorry, Ms. Bina. This is Mendi, a new friend I met." Gesturing impatiently for Mendi to come and introduce himself, the young man walked up to Ms. Bina's extended hand and shook it.

"Ms. Bina, I am so sorry to come intruding into your home like this, but I have been waiting for all your guests to leave so I could speak with you and Yona alone. I have some very serious news I overheard and I don't know who else to tell," Mendi explained. "As you can see, I am quite on edge about this and need to talk to someone. I'm new in this village and have only really spoken to Yona and Cobar, of course."

At the mention of Cobar's name, Ms. Bina withdrew her hand as a scowl came over her face.

"You best explain yourself, young man," Ms. Bina warned him. "I am not a friend of Cobar and I hope you are not either."

"Oh no! Cobar is not my friend. I just came here looking to get a job with him."

"If you are working for Cobar, then I suggest you leave here immediately. We have nothing to say to you. His son, Zelig, has already been here once and that is enough!"

"No. You don't understand. I'm here to warn you about what Cobar and a man named Hamah are planning to do!"

"I already know what Cobar is planning to do!" Ms. Bina replied sternly. Yona realized that Ms. Bina was not going to listen unless she intervened.

112

"Ms. Bina, I met Mendi before he went to speak with Cobar, and he offered to see what he could do to help me. I think we should hear what he has to say."

Still unsure about Mendi's motives, Ms. Bina agreed.

"Oh, thank you so much! I just don't know what else to do!" Mendi responded.

"Well, why don't you start by sitting down and having a sip of tea before you begin," Ms. Bina suggested. "Yona, would you mind serving some tea to our guest?"

Though the woman was cordial enough, she had her reasons for encouraging Mendi to drink some tea. She figured the herbs would help clear his mind and settle his nerves so he could better communicate with them. While Yona was preparing the tea, Ms. Haddie had a few questions for him while he waited.

"So Mendi," she began, "before you tell us what you have heard, I am going to tell you what I saw so there will be nothing concealed between us."

"You saw something?" he asked. "I thought you couldn't see and that's why Yona was brought here."

"It's true," she responded. "I can't see with my natural eyes, but I can see in a different way as Elemet directs."

Just as Mendi was preparing to ask another question, Yona returned with the tea. Though in the kitchen, she had overheard their conversation. As she handed Mendi his cup of tea, she explained.

"Ms. Bina can see things when someone holds her hand."

"What? I've never heard of that before," he responded.

"I'm sure there are a great many things that we are aware of that you have never heard of before," Ms. Bina replied. "So let me tell you what I saw."

Ms. Bina accurately depicted Mendi's job interview with Cobar and then gave a brief summary of him overhearing the conversation between Cobar and Hamah.

"That is amazing!" Mendi exclaimed. "So you saw all that when I shook your hand?"

"Yes. So I know you are connected with Cobar. That makes me very suspicious," Ms. Bina answered.

By that time Yona had taken her seat next to Ms. Bina and grabbed hold of her hand so she could see Mendi for herself.

"She can see what has happened in the past, but can't actually hear what is being said," Yona added. Just as she was about to give further information about Ms. Bina's gift, another voice was heard coming from the bedroom area of the house.

"Bina might not be able to hear everything that was said in the past, but I certainly can," the woman's voice said.

In shock, all three of them turned and looked in the direction of the voice. Stepping out from the shadows of the darkened bedroom was Miss Haddie.

"Haddie!" Ms. Bina exclaimed in joy. "I'm so glad you are here. What a surprise!"

Unsure of who the woman was, Mendi immediately stood, still wondering how this woman had entered the cabin without being seen or heard. Her presence made him nervous, but somehow he knew she would have the wisdom they needed to deal with the information he carried.

"Hello sister! It is so good to see you again." Continuing her walk towards the group, she approached Yona first and gave her a big hug. "Dear girl, it is so wonderful to finally meet you in person. I am hopeful that Jessah may stop by to see you again at another time," she explained. "She was busy with another assignment this evening."

"Oh, it would be wonderful to see Jessah again!" Yona replied, beaming with joy.

Next Miss Haddie went over to her sister, patting her hand and giving her a little kiss on the cheek. "So how is my big sister holding up with all this?" she asked with a smile.

"I am holding up just fine," Ms. Bina said, "especially since you are here to help us sort this mess out. Have you met Mendi yet?"

"No, I have not met him before," she said while approaching the young man. "So, this is the one who is becoming our informant. Hello, Mendi. So glad to meet you." Miss Haddie held out her hand to shake, but Mendi was nervous.

"So, if your sister can see things when she holds people's hands, what happens if I hold your hand?"

"Why don't you shake my hand and find out?" Miss Haddie encouraged him.

Unsure about it, Mendi glanced over at Yona for reassurance. Yona nodded encouragingly. Finally, Mendi grabbed her hand. The moment he did, a jolt of light went through him sending him backwards into his chair. Ms. Bina and Yona laughed as he looked quite shocked.

"What was that?" he asked.

"Oh, just a little internal housecleaning," Miss Haddie explained. "You will be fine. So, now that I'm here, I think we all would like to hear your description of what you heard earlier today. Bina and Yona need to hear this for themselves. Proceed."

Nodding, it took Mendi several minutes to gather his thoughts so he could accurately report all he had heard at the inn as the women sat and listened.

Chapter Nineteen

GETTING IN POSITION

Nervously, Uri stood before the archway swallowing in hopes of moistening his dry throat. Behind him, his friends offered encouragement as he prepared to walk through the portal leading to his first assignment since arriving at the Eagles' Nest. He had grown accustomed to the support of his new family, but the time had come for him to step out on his own, relying on the voice of Elemet.

"You can do this," Galen reassured him.

"I suppose so, or Chen would not have asked me to go," Uri replied. "Okay. I'm going to do it. I will see all of you on the other side of this quest."

"Yes, for sure," Roany responded. "We will be together again at some point."

Seeing his hesitation, Shoshanna walked up to Uri one more time and beckoned for him to lean over. As he did, she gave him a hug and a quick kiss upon his cheek.

"Remember how loved you are," she said. "And go love all those children with the grace you have been given. Those orphans need you."

"They do need me," Uri admitted. "Thank you, my friends!" With that comment, Uri boldly stepped forward through the archway and disappeared from view.

Recalling the instructions he had been given, Uri paused before taking the next step which placed him before the heavy wooden doors of Camp Shabelle. For a brief moment all the terrible memories of loneliness, rejection, and fear tried to flood his mind, even as the haze attempted to saturate his lungs.

As the battle began, Uri felt warmth radiating from the cheek Shoshanna had kissed prior to his departure. Her words resounded in his mind, reminding him that he was no longer that rejected and fearful little boy, but a new man.

"I am loved!" he repeated. "I am loved, and I will love these children." Even as he made that declaration, a fresh wave of Elemet's love washed over him. Confidence arose as Uri approached the front doors and entered as the man he had become.

Uri boldly moved toward the receptionist.

"Hi, I am Uriah. I was sent here by one of the village elders because they had heard Camp Shabelle was in need of additional help."

"Oh?" she responded. "And which village elder was that?"

"His name is Mahaz from the village of Ruel," Uri replied recalling the script he had practiced so many times at the Eagles' Nest. "Mahaz told me after one of the recent village elders' meetings, it was mentioned that Camp

Shabelle was looking for additional staff. He sent me here saying my size and strength would be a benefit to you."

"Well, yes," she admitted. "We do have quite a few tasks that require strength. Would you mind waiting here while I summon Miss Moselle? She is the one who makes those types of decisions." Standing up from her desk, the woman headed across the entryway, but stopped for a moment.

"What did you say your name was again?" she asked.

"Uriah. I'm Uriah sent by Mahaz, the village elder."

"Okay. I will be right back."

As soon as she was out of sight, Uri took a good look around the entryway. Yes, the cold stone walls still appeared the same as when he lived there. Chilled by the drop in temperature, Uri wrapped his coat a little tighter around his body as he waited. Though he knew this place was filled with children, he heard no laughter or running feet as he had grown accustomed to in the Eagles' Nest these last several weeks. This saddened him, but remembering why he was there, Uri felt a new determination rise up within.

He would not abandon them nor the purpose for which he was sent.

The clicking of shoes walking on hard floors alerted him of the two approaching ladies; one was the receptionist and the other, Miss Moselle, director of Camp Shabelle. The receptionist passed right by him returning to her desk almost smirking as she anticipated the upcoming interrogation. She knew what was coming.

Suspicious, the older woman moved in to get some answers as to who sent him to her domain without the

119

customary message announcing his arrival. Looking over the applicant and taking note of his size, she had to admit, he would fill a need she had for greater security. He certainly looked intimidating enough. What puzzled her was why Cobar had not responded directly to her request several weeks ago. Miss Moselle finally spoke.

"So Mahaz sent you?" she questioned him.

"Yes, ma'am," he replied unflinchingly.

"Why is it that I have never heard of him before?" she asked while looking for any sign of nervousness.

"His father recently passed away and because Mahaz had been under his training at the time, he was asked to fill that position right away," Uri replied, grateful that he had rehearsed his responses so often, they came out easily.

"Hmm. Well, I guess that makes sense, though I do expect Cobar and this Mahaz to follow proper protocol in the future. I will certainly remind Cobar of this the next time I speak with him," Miss Moselle conceded. "So your name is Uriah?"

"Yes, Uriah."

"And what experience do you have as a security guard?" she pressed him.

"Well, I've worked with other security guards in the past and am very familiar with how things are run," he stated. "I'm sure I can figure out what is needed here and adapt quickly."

"Very well then, Uriah," she replied, satisfied with his answer. "Why don't you follow me to my office where I can explain how things are run here at Camp Shabelle."

As she led the way down the hall, Uri took a deep breath of relief. Miss Moselle obviously did not recognize him and soon he would be able to begin his assignment as security for the orphanage. He had to snicker as he thought about his past "experience" in working with security guards. As a detained inmate in several prisons, Uri had become quite familiar with the security guards before he ran into Galen. Now he was given the chance to bring a different kind of security into the lives of orphans who were stuck in this cold, hard place.

With Uri already positioned at Camp Shabelle, the three friends knew their own time was drawing near, but before they were to leave, another dear friend was getting ready to depart. Galen, Shoshanna, and Roany rushed over to one of the rolling hills where Azriel and his team would be taking flight on the back of the golden eagles they had trained with. Family and friends gathered as the gallant aerial warriors prepared for their launch.

After carefully checking the supplies in each of their knapsacks, the warriors listened to final instructions given by Azriel as to where they would land prior to the morning of the attack. The plan was to camp overnight on one of the ridges so they could observe the movements of the enforcers below them. At the appointed time the following morning, they would begin the first of their assaults on Camp Coshek.

Though outwardly calm, Azriel was fighting nervousness. While Galen and Roany stepped up close to admire the many golden eagles assembled to fly the warriors to their vantage point, Shoshanna approached Azriel when she noticed he was alone.

"Hi. I wanted you to know, I think you are very brave to do this."

"Well, thank you. I have to admit, I don't feel very brave at the moment, but I'm sure it will kick in shortly," Azriel responded as he closed up his knapsack.

"We just saw Uri off to Camp Shabelle," Shoshanna informed him. "He was a little nervous, but pressed through it. I know you will as well."

"Thank you. Do you know when you will be heading out?"

"I think we are also leaving soon, but I don't know exactly when. Chen spoke with us and gave us some directions on what we will be doing," Shoshanna explained.

Just then Galen and Roany returned from examining the eagles.

"Wow!" Roany exclaimed. "The beaks and claws on those eagles are massive! It's a good thing they are pets."

"Well, either they have become our pets or we have become theirs!" Azriel replied with a laugh. "However it is, we work well together." Speaking to all three of his friends, Azriel encouraged them to come meet his personal eagle up close. The great eagle flapped his wings in excitement as they approached.

"Hey, Zuko," Azriel said with his hands extended towards the eagle's face. "Relax, buddy. We'll be leaving

Getting in Position

soon, but first I want you to meet my friends." As soon as Azriel drew near, the eagle calmed down allowing his rider to gently stroke the golden feathers on his head. Once he was settled, Azriel called them over. Shoshanna gravitated to his head and wise eyes while Galen and Roany laid their hands upon his strong wings and glistening body.

Zuko kept his eyes upon the men at his side, but once he looked upon Shoshanna, he bowed his head allowing her to peer directly into his eyes. She saw no fear, but a strong confidence and trust, especially between him and Azriel.

"He trusts you," Shoshanna said. "I can see he is quite confident."

"Oh yes," Azriel replied while still rubbing his head affectionately. "Confident and a little head-strong at times. He knows what he wants to do and occasionally ignores my instructions on where to fly, but we've learned to work together. Right, Zuko?"

Shortly Galen and Roany joined them beside the great bird's head and after giving Zuka one more pat, they decided it was time to retreat so Azriel could finish his final preparations. Before the three friends had gotten too far, Azriel decided to reveal something he was beginning to sense.

"There is a possibility I may not return from this mission, but I wanted all three of you to know that I have seen something very unique in you. You carry a light that appears very different from others I have seen. Elemet has called you for this mission. You are more prepared than you realize right now. It has been an honor to get to know you and call you my friends."

Galen immediately walked up to Azriel and extended his hand in appreciation.

"Thank you for your example and integrity. Your dedication is an inspiration to us all. Be strong and courageous, my friend." Right after Galen released his hand, Roany also shook Azriel's hand.

"Azriel, you are a man of honor yourself. We'll see you on the other side of this journey one way or another." As Roany stepped back, Azriel extended his hand to Shoshanna as well. Rather than grabbing his hand, Shoshanna gave him a hug.

"You and Zuko make darkness shudder. Whichever way things go, Elemet has a plan, and it is always perfect. Thank you for being our friend," Shoshanna smiled.

As she stepped back beside Galen, he grabbed her hand. Together they stood and watched as Azriel mounted the golden eagle and the two of them flew as one, leading his warriors and the other eagles to their destined location.

A single tear flowed down Shoshanna's cheek as she watched them disappear in the distance. Suddenly, she turned and embraced Galen as she thought of Azriel and his men flying off to face the darkness attempting to choke out the island of Kumani. With her head buried in his chest, she looked up at him and asked.

"Do you think they will all return?"

"I honestly don't know," Galen responded, "but whether they return here or move on to the place where Elemet dwells, someday we will see them again."

After a few moments of silence, Galen put his arm around Shoshanna as they walked back with Roany, knowing that soon they too would be sent out on their own mission to accomplish all they had been prepared to do.

Chapter Twenty

A SCRAMBLE FOR POWER

"There's much more to life than you've known." The words of Miss Haddie resonated in his head as Mendi opened his eyes. Suddenly all that had transpired over the last several days came back to him: the terrifying words of Hamah; the lengthy tea party held at Ms. Bina's house; and finally his opportunity to tell someone what he had overheard.

His heart raced in panic.

While still gaining clarity from a sleep-induced fog, he recalled Miss Haddie's dramatic entrance from "nowhere" and the wise counsel she offered as they discussed what needed to happen. The next days were spent with Ms. Bina and Yona. They shared all they knew about Elemet in the daylight hours. In the evenings, Miss Haddie would "pop in" to continue Mendi's rapid training and instruction in the ways of the eagle. He still didn't understand how she suddenly appeared from Ms. Bina's room and she offered no explanation.

Time was of the essence!

Yes, he definitely was ready to surrender all things to Elemet, especially since he knew what lay ahead of him if he did not. Someone bigger than himself needed to direct his actions if he and the rest of Kumani were to survive this enslavement!

Taking a deep breath, Mendi knew he needed to calm himself so he could clearly recollect the plans for that day and play his role efficiently. Silently calling out to Elemet for assistance, he felt a blanket of peace and love fall upon him. As he drank in this refreshing, he suddenly saw the plan they had discussed appear before his closed eyes. With great interest, he observed his part in the arrangement. He already felt better.

"Time to get up," he told himself. "I can do this!"

Within a short period of time, Mendi was dressed, enjoyed a cup of Miss Haddie's tea, and headed out the door of the inn where he was staying. As he walked, he noticed the light before him directing his steps, just as Miss Haddie had described. This gave him great hope that he could pull off what he had been sent to do.

Confidently, Mendi opened the door of the print shop, expecting to see Cobar as he had before, but his desk sat vacant. Though the bell had rung as he entered, no one responded.

"Cobar? Are you here?" he called out. With no one answering either the bell or his call, he decided to step around the front counter and peek in through the back door to the shop itself. Pushing the door open just enough to see if someone were close by, he noticed the presses sitting abandoned and quiet.

The light clearly directed him to enter the back of the shop, so he cautiously followed where it led. Though he had just met Cobar a couple of days earlier, the stories both Yona and Ms. Bina shared let him know this was not a man to trifle with. After only five minutes of wandering through the shop, Mendi was ready to turn back, however the light indicated he needed to continue. Not wanting to risk failing his new friends and Elemet himself, Mendi decided to press on just a little further.

With his nerves on edge, Mendi took one more step when suddenly one of the small backrooms lit up. Obviously, someone was there, so Mendi approached the door and knocked lightly. Immediately, the candle was blown out causing the room to darken once more.

Knocking a second time, he identified himself, hoping he would be allowed to enter.

"It's me, Mendi," he said, just loud enough to be heard. "I am looking for Cobar. I have some good news to report."

Slowly the door opened as Cobar emerged with a smile.

"Oh, Mendi," he said. "I was not expecting you. My son and I were just having a private meeting back here. So, you have some good news for me?"

"Yes. I was able to befriend Ms. Bina as you asked. These last couple of days, I've been able to get to know her pretty well," Mendi replied with a smile.

"Oh yes! Ms. Bina. That's right. Now I remember. So did you learn anything important?"

"Well, I know she is still blind and Yona is continuing to help her," Mendi reported.

"Yona?" Zelig uttered while pushing his way out of the darkened office to stand next to his father. "You spent some time with my Yona?"

"Zelig! Calm down! He is only doing what I sent him to do," Cobar reminded his son. "And she is not *your* Yona yet."

"Oh!" Mendi feigned surprise. "I thought Yona was only twelve years old. Why was a twelve-year-old added to the list of available women?"

"She is a special case," Cobar explained nervously. "An orphan. Anyway, we have much more pressing matters to discuss now."

"But father, how am I to still get Yona with all these changes going on?" Zelig complained.

"Zelig, stop! I have some very important business I want you to attend to," and then taking a moment to size up Mendi, he added, "And I could use your help as well, Mendi."

"And what about the threat from Ms. Bina?" he asked with a concerned expression.

"No, no, no! She's not our concern right now," Cobar corrected him. Clearing his throat nervously, he continued. "A couple of days ago, an acquaintance visited me. I know he left our village, but I want you to find out where he went from here. I need to know."

"Well, I'm not really a tracker or outdoorsman, if you know what I mean," Mendi replied. "How am I supposed to find out where he is?"

129

"You can check with the people in the surrounding villages to see if they have seen him," Cobar suggested. "I don't think he went very far. His name is Hamah."

At the mention of Hamah's name, Mendi's stomach tightened. He knew very well who this man was and even had an idea of what he looked like. This was not someone Mendi would want to run into if he could help it.

"Oh yeah, Hamah!" Zelig chimed in. "Great guy! When you find him, send him our greetings."

Turning in irritation towards his son, Cobar's scowl let Zelig know he was not to say any more.

"And you, my dear son, have the task of notifying the village elders that we have an emergency meeting coming up later this week. You can send out enforcers to help you contact them."

"When I find him, should I let Hamah know about this meeting as well?" Mendi asked.

"No! Do not let Hamah know about this at all!" Cobar responded in panic. Realizing he had revealed some of his own fears, he quickly added, "We have some surprises planned for our visitor and don't want to ruin it for him."

"Oh sure! I can understand that," Mendi smiled. "How soon do you want me to start looking for him?"

"Right away. The sooner you find him, the sooner we can let all the village elders know about our plans," Cobar replied.

"I guess I can do that," Mendi answered. "I will just need some time to pack up my knapsack. I'll let you know as soon as I find him." Nodding, Mendi headed back out towards the front office. As he left, he could hear Zelig discussing his instructions with his father.

"And how am I supposed to contact the village elders without running across Hamah?"

"You can figure that out for yourself!" Cobar replied gruffly.

With Cobar and Zelig still in the back room of the print shop, Mendi decided to take a detour and report what he had learned to Ms. Bina and Yona before packing up for his journey. He approached their back door to avoid being seen and knocked. Shortly Yona appeared and welcomed him in.

"So how did it go?" Ms. Bina inquired.

"Well, it's obvious that Hamah has terrified Cobar," he began. "I found both Cobar and his son having a private meeting in the back room of the print shop. He only opened the door to speak with me when I mentioned I had 'good news' for him."

"As far as to what I learned, Cobar definitely has other things on his mind right now and really is not worried about you at this moment, however, Zelig was very concerned that I had spent some time with you, Yona."

"Who does he think he is?" Yona snapped. "I don't belong to him!"

"That's true," Mendi replied, "but he did refer to you as 'my Yona.' When I mentioned that you were only twelve,

Cobar just said you were an orphan and this was a special case."

"Those two are both snakes, along with that fiend, Hamah!" Ms. Bina declared before continuing. "So, are you going to look for Hamah as Cobar requested? I don't know if that is wise."

"Yes," Yona chimed in. "I don't think you should mess with Hamah at all."

"Well, I'm not planning on messing with him—just locating him. I feel like I need to stay on Cobar's good side, if he has one," Mendi added sarcastically. "If I can report Hamah's location to him, I can continue reporting Cobar's activities to both of you and Miss Haddie."

"But how are you going to track him?" Yona asked worriedly.

"After spending all that time in training with you and Miss Haddie, I now know that I really have an unfair advantage in tracking Hamah."

"And what is that?" Yona asked.

"I just follow the light to see where he is staying and report his location to Cobar," Mendi replied with a smile.

"I don't know, dear," Ms. Bina responded. "You make it sound so easy. With the intensity of darkness this Hamah is walking in, he probably has lots of security around him. It seems like the enforcers traveling with him could be a threat, and you might face possible imprisonment if they see you."

"That is true, but if we never step out and use the resources we have been given, then darkness and the haze have already defeated us. I was trained by all of you for a reason. I feel as though Elemet is calling me to move out and trust him. I have to do this," he declared.

Upon hearing his decision, Yona walked over to Mendi and gave him a hug. "Your courage is inspiring. Whatever happens, I want you to know that you are amazing. Thanks for being my friend."

"And don't you dare leave without coming over here and hugging me as well," Ms. Bina added.

Suddenly Yona stopped and looked back at Ms. Bina.

"Did you see me hugging Mendi?" she asked.

"I suppose I did!" Ms. Bina answered, a little surprised herself. "I forgot I was no longer holding your hand. Oh, my stars! I can see!"

"Really?" Yona responded excitedly. "Tell me what I am doing now."

"You are waving your hands and Mendi is still standing beside you, not moving over here to give me a hug!" she responded. "Come on, Mendi! It's my turn now."

Mendi came over and quickly hugged Ms. Bina.

"Oh, I'm so glad I can see again!" Ms. Bina declared. "Now I can take better aim at that Zelig's head with my cane if he dare show up here again!"

"Well, I wouldn't suggest that," Mendi responded. "In fact, maybe you should consider playing blind whenever others are around. That way you can take note of what they are really doing without them knowing it. Besides, if they know you are no longer blind, that may just be another excuse for Cobar to speed up the process for Zelig to get Yona."

"Not on your life!" Yona replied. "I'd rather be living in the woods alone than married to that Zelig."

"Well then, let's keep Ms. Bina's new vision to ourselves for now. At least that might buy us some time so I can be around to help fight him off!"

"Really?" Yona asked. "You would fight Zelig off for me?"

"If it came to that, I would."

"Thank you, Mendi!" she said.

"You're welcome, Yona."

Realizing Ms. Bina was now watching their every move, Mendi was feeling a little uncomfortable and decided it might be best if he hurried back to his room in the inn to pack. He wanted to begin his journey while it was still daylight so he could arrive at the next village before nightfall.

Chapter Twenty-One

A HOME INSTEAD

After several days of traveling, Oren and Tanzi were exhausted when they finally arrived at Eber and Giza's homestead. It had been a difficult trip, especially with her cart full of supplies and the things she had salvaged from her home. Avoiding enforcers with just a knapsack on your back was much easier than doing so with a cart. However, by following the direction of the light before them, they were able to end their journey without any mishaps.

Both Eber and Giza hurried out to greet them, especially when they saw their old friend, Tanzi.

"Oren! Tanzi! Welcome!" Giza called out. "What a thrill to see both of you!" Giza headed straight for Tanzi and embraced her excitedly. "Oren has kept us informed of all that has occurred in your life recently. We are so happy you are here for a visit!"

"Well, actually," Oren interjected, "this might be more than just a visit."

Eber stepped closer, curious to hear what Oren had to say. "What has happened?" he asked.

"While I was escorting Tanzi to Ms. Bina's tea party, she had some unexpected visitors come to her cabin," Oren explained. "They tore her place up looking for some information, we think."

"Oh Tanzi, that is terrible!" Giza remarked.

"Were they able to find anything of value?" Eber inquired.

"We don't think so. Tanzi, very wisely decided to keep the important papers with her when we left," Oren smiled. "After we saw the condition of her cabin, we knew it was time for her to move to a safer place. That's why we are here. Eber, Giza, how do you feel about housing an old friend of yours for a time?"

"Oh, that would be wonderful!" Giza gushed.

Looking directly at Eber, Oren checked to see if he was equally open to housing Tanzi.

"Tanzi, it would be an honor to have you join us on this homestead," Eber stated. "Besides, both Giza and I would love to hear your firsthand account of meeting Chen. We also had a wonderful encounter ourselves."

"Enough talking," Giza interrupted. "You must be tired. Please come in and relax for a bit. I'll brew some tea and pull out some fresh biscuits for all of us to enjoy while we hear of your journey."

Before entering the cottage, Oren glanced behind Eber and Giza's home and noticed something he had not seen before—a guest house similar to the one he had on Miss Haddie's homestead. He also noticed that their property appeared larger than he remembered. Puzzled by this, he decided to ask Eber about it later.

As usual, it was quite late when Jessah stepped into Camp Shabelle. This had been her regular routine several nights a week. Malia always woke up easily and quickly followed Jessah to a safe place where they could talk. Every time Jessah returned, Malia had wonderful reports on how the other children were responding to the truths she was bringing to them. Word had spread among the orphans and nearly every one of them eagerly gravitated to hearing about the ways of the eagle Malia that shared with them. In this dark place, the light of truth shown quite brightly!

As Jessah moved quietly along the familiar corridors leading to the girls' dorm, she heard the jingle of keys echoing down one of the hallways. Quickly, she hid herself in the shadows and watched to see who might be moving around at this hour. Her eyes strained to see down the darkened hallway, but she could only make out the dim outline of a man moving in her direction.

She held her breath as he drew closer, afraid to make any kind of movement. However, as he approached, she noticed something very familiar about him. His body seemed to have a slight glow about it and as she studied his face, her fears melted away immediately. Taking a step out from the shadows, with a smile on her face, Jessah boldly stood before the man.

He stopped and stared for a moment, wondering who this young, wandering child was. Then it dawned on him.

"Jessah! What are you doing here? I thought you were living with Miss Haddie."

"Oh, I am living with her," she said. "I visit here at night. And what are you doing here? The last time I saw you, you were all heading towards the Eagles' Nest. Did you make it there?"

Now Uri was smiling. "Oh yes. We made it there and then we were immediately trained for placement where we would be needed. And, this is where Chen asked me to come."

"You look a little different," Jessah commented, "I'm not sure what it is."

"Yes, the change was necessary," Uri answered. "I heard that my name and drawings of me had been circulated throughout the villages, so Chen changed my appearance and asked me to go by the name of Uriah when I applied for this position."

"And what is your position?" she asked.

"I am the new security officer."

Giggling, Jessah replied, "Of course you are! I'm sure that will be very helpful when it comes time for me to finish what I have been assigned to do."

"What are you assigned to do?"

"Well, for now I am meeting with Malia and teaching her the ways of the eagle. Malia has been sharing what I teach her with the other children. The last time I saw her, she said the other children were responding to the truth. They are being prepared, and I believe Elemet sent you here to help us at the appointed time."

"I can see that," Uri answered, "but you'll have to tell me what is being planned."

"Oh, I will, but Elemet asked me to not let anyone know what he is planning until the time is right," she said. "Until then, I guess I will be seeing you on the nights I come to meet with Malia. You should probably let her know that we are friends and tell her you are here to help. That will encourage her. I will tell her as well."

"Great. So you met with Elemet?"

"Yes, but I will have to tell you about that another time," she replied. "I need to go awaken Malia right now so I can get back to Miss Haddie's home before dawn."

"Wait! How do you travel that quickly through the woods at night?"

"How did you get here from the Eagles' Nest?" she asked.

Uri thought for a moment. "Oh! You go through that doorway like I did?"

"Yes. I really like that doorway! Don't you?"

"Oh yes. That was very fast and easy. Okay. I better continue my rounds while you finish your meeting with Malia."

"Great. See you next time, Uriah," Jessah smiled as she walked the other direction.

As she left, Uri couldn't help but wonder about her meeting with Elemet and just exactly what he had planned for Camp Shabelle. Whatever it was, it excited him to know that he was to have a part in it. Continuing his security check, Uri moved down the hallway, checking doors and locks as was his usual routine at night. As he approached the mess hall, he suddenly noticed the smell of smoke and saw lights dancing on the walls of the darkened room. Suspecting a fire, Uri rushed into the room to see what had happened.

Instead of an uncontrollable fire, Uri spotted the figure of a man sitting comfortably in a substantial chair next to the brightly burning fire in the large fireplace. Grabbing the club hanging at his side, he approached the intruder, trying to appear as threatening as possible.

"Sir, I don't know who you are, but you have no business here in Camp Shabelle, especially at this time of night," Uri said in his sternest voice of authority. "I need to ask you to leave immediately!" Unresponsive to Uri's request, the man simply took another sip of his tea while staring at the flames before him.

Surprised by the intruder's indifference, Uri wondered if the man could hear him, so he made his way across the mess hall to visibly confront the uninvited visitor. As the light cast by the fire illuminated the face of the stranger, Uri took a better look at the man who was obviously ignoring him. He stopped in his tracks, startled by what he saw.

"Chen! What are you doing here?"

"Oh, I thought I might stop by and see how you were doing," Chen replied with a smile. "Would you like to join me for a cup of Miss Haddie's tea? It is most refreshing."

As Uri stood, momentarily mesmerized by his friend's glowing face and vibrant eyes, he suddenly realized that Chen had asked him a question.

"Oh! Well, I am supposed to be completing my security check right about now."

"All is secure and taken care of for you, my friend. Come! Sit down and join me," Chen encouraged him.

Still in shock, Uri glanced around for a place to sit and noticed that a second chair had appeared alongside Chen's with another cup of steaming tea sitting on a small table between the two chairs. With all his concerns laid aside, the large man sat, picked up the warm mug, and enjoyed a sip of the sweetly spiced brew filling his senses.

The two sat briefly in silence while staring at the light show projecting from the frolicking flames. A great peace and refreshing washed over Uri just knowing that Chen was here, even in this cold, dark place. Finally, Chen spoke.

"I am so pleased with your great courage to return to the place you once hated. Though there are challenges here, I know you can see the great treasure that is currently locked within its confines."

"Treasure?" Uri asked. "What treasure are you speaking of?"

"The children are my treasure!"

A little puzzled by his response, Uri turned towards him inquiringly. "How are the children your treasure?"

"The truth is that every individual on Kumani was designed and created by my father, Elemet, with a portion of himself placed within them from the moment they were conceived. Once born, each child grows in understanding until they are able to make choices between listening to truth or to lies regarding who they are and where they came from," Chen explained.

"As you have seen for yourself, Kumani is full of many lies and deceptions designed to prevent the people here from making wise choices based on truth as opposed to fear. The time has come for this deception to be exposed so that every individual can freely choose for themselves. That is why you are here."

"How is my presence going to help achieve that?" Uri asked.

"You are at Camp Shabelle to help guard and escort my great treasures to their freedom."

"I don't understand how I can do that," Uri responded, even more puzzled than before.

"You don't need to understand how to do this," Chen replied, "as you will hear your instructions at the proper time. However, you do need to understand how valuable these young children are. They have been placed here to indoctrinate them into a lifestyle of fear and deception. Once they have grown and are released into the villages, they were meant to be full supporters of the current system, enabling control to continue."

Shaken by this truth, Uri had to ask, "And I was to be one of their staunch supporters as well?"

"Yes, but instead of submitting, your anger towards injustice rose up. Your strength of character told you that another truth existed. That is when you met Galen and your journey back to trust, innocence, and great love began."

"So, you still haven't explained how the children at Camp Shabelle are your great treasures," Uri persisted. Nodding, Chen continued.

"The children here are still in their formative years. And, though the indoctrination continues, one of my champions has arisen in their midst who releases truth to these hungry captives. As the truth comes forth, some will eagerly grab onto it, rejecting the lies."

"And, who is this champion?"

"Oh, you know her," Chen responded with a grin.

"Jessah?"

"Yes. Because of her child-like trust in Elemet, Jessah has been granted the privilege of seeing others, like herself, set free from every lie. The children's fearlessness and unlimited joy will create great ripples across this island, causing many things to change. These young ones are your hope for a different future."

"So, how do I guard your treasures?"

"You love them and affirm the truths that have been presented," Chen replied. "These children need to know that there are adults who do know the truth and will not allow delusional people, like Miss Moselle, to abuse or rob my children prior to their release."

"And, how do I do that?"

"Oh, don't you worry," Chen assured him. "When the time comes, you will hear Elemet as he gives you instructions, and our light will lead you."

"You are the source of that light?" Uri asked, quite surprised.

"Yes. I am the way you need to go, the truth that gives you understanding, and the only way to truly live life." Directly after Chen had spoken these words, Uri noticed the fire was quickly diminishing. After looking into the dying flames, Uri glanced back towards Chen and discovered both he and his chair had vanished. Standing to take a better look around, Uri's own chair and the table also faded from sight.

Once again, the mess hall was dark and all was silent.

Shaking his head in amazement, Uri exited the room. As he walked out, a new voice echoed in his head. "Guard my treasure. I will direct your every step."

Chapter Twenty-Two

A HIGHER PERSPECTIVE

Circling high above the island of Kumani, Azriel's team rode upon the backs of the great golden eagles, looking down upon Camp Coshek. From their vantage point they could see the layout and activities of the camp. With Hamah preoccupied with his plans for the villages and their elders in the lowlands, most of his drug-induced enforcers had been required to take up their duties elsewhere. Only a skeleton crew were left to maintain the smoldering fires and the contaminating of the waters soon to be released into the lakes, creeks, and rivers throughout the island.

The first wave of contamination had already been released, but when the second wave hit, those without Hamah's antidote would quickly find themselves engulfed in confusion and weakness. If left unchecked, the combination of new toxins filling the air and the tainted waters they drank would ultimately lead to their deaths. Azriel, aware of Hamah's devious plan, took great caution to avoid being seen by those still caring for the camp.

Spotting a high plateau above Camp Coshek, Azriel motioned for his team to land so they could establish their camp, well out of sight. The army of eagles silently lit upon the plateau allowing their riders to slide off. The men began setting up tents and other provisions so they could use their vantage point to observe the activities below. Once the men and their supplies were removed from their rides, the eagles extended their wings, once again catching the wind and headed back towards the Eagles' Nest. The eagles would return when their services were needed again.

Azriel was the first to slowly move to the edge of the ridge where he could observe the men below. With great caution, he positioned himself in a manner that would not dislodge any of the loose stones around him. He and his men did not want to draw attention to themselves in any way.

Soon, Keoni, one of his team members, slid up beside Azriel to discuss their first plan of action.

"How does it look down there?"

"From what I can see, there only appears to be a small group of enforcers left behind to continue sending the haze into the lowlands. My guess is that the reservoir contains the waters to be released for the second contamination Chen told me about," Azriel replied, as he studied the movements below.

"So what are we going to do?" Keoni asked.

"First, we need to find a way down to the camp from here and then see if we can access that reservoir before the toxins are released into the waters of Kumani."

"And what of the smoke?"

146

"We have a plan for that as well, but first the water must be taken care of," Azriel answered. "Can I entrust you with the responsibility of finding a trail down to the reservoir? I need to meet with the other men to discuss our plan of action."

"I would be honored to help with that. Should I go alone?"

"Why don't you take Gabor with you?" Azriel suggested. "He is quite a gifted tracker and would be a help to you."

"Yes. I will get him and begin our exploration immediately."

"Just make sure you both make it back to our campsite before nightfall so we can make our plans for the morning."

"We will."

Azriel took his eyes off Camp Coshek to study his friend for a moment before he left. "Keoni, you are a good man. May the wisdom and strength of Elemet go with you both."

"Thank you, Azriel. We will see you tonight!"

Watching as Keoni hurried off, Azriel took a deep breath, realizing the danger he was placing his friends in. After taking one more final glance at the facility below, he withdrew from the ledge to join the other team members completing the set up for the night. As much as he would prefer to be the one facing all the risks, he knew they were a team, needing to work together to accomplish all that was being asked of them. Their combined success was critical to the survival of the residents of Kumani.

The two scouts headed out from their observation post and down the rough terrain, doing their best to avoid the loose rock and gravel they encountered while searching the brush around them. As Gabor pushed aside some low-hanging tree branches, he gestured to get Keoni's attention. Quietly, Keoni joined his friend. Though quite overgrown, a trail had been found.

"It was most likely used by animals traveling these parts," Gabor explained, "but it will work for us."

"Great! Let's see if it ends up near the camp."

It was already mid-morning by the time they found the trail, so both men knew it would have to be a quick journey down and back so they could report back to Azriel before nightfall. The knapsacks on their backs carried water, some equipment, and just enough food for a one-day journey. If they were delayed in any way, they would have to wait until morning before returning to their post so as to avoid either missing the trail completely or slipping on the rock as they tried to climb back up.

The two men worked together skillfully, using ropes to assist in their trek. They worked as quietly as they could, realizing that any commotion might arouse the attention of the enforcers who were maintaining both the fire and the septic waters of the reservoir.

It was mid-afternoon before Keoni indicated he needed a water break. Both men were glad to sit for a moment and eat some of the bread and cheese they had brought for the journey. Not much was said as they sat on a fallen log in the forest region now surrounding them. Breathing heavily, Keoni drank the cool water from the gourd. Some of the water ran down his chin bringing delightful coolness to his chest.

"How close do you think we are?" he asked Gabor.

"I'm guessing we must be pretty close now. We should probably veer a little west so we can watch for the camp."

Just as Gabor had responded, both men heard some movement in the region around them, so they quickly took cover. Holding their breaths, they peered through the trees and watched as two enforcers walked the perimeter of Camp Coshek. They were so close, they could see glimpses of the familiar blue shirts Hamah's enforcers often wore. The first man spoke.

"Did you add the last of the toxins to the water already?" he asked.

"Yes. It has already been poured in. It's only a matter of time before the poison mixes with the other toxins. Tomorrow I will test the waters one more time before we release it, just to make sure everything is mixed thoroughly, as Hamah instructed."

"Good! Lord Hamah will certainly be in his proper position of authority tomorrow, and all of us will be ruling right along with him," the first man replied with a smile. "I'm certain that he will replace us with others who can maintain the haze and waters exactly as he desires. We are quickly approaching the day he has told us about."

"Yes. We are living in an exciting season," the second man agreed.

"Alright. Let's head back now. Everything is prepared and ready to go."

After waiting a safe period of time, Keoni and Gabor moved toward the area where the two enforcers had just been. Slowly, they pushed back the branches.

A huge reservoir of green-looking water lay before them. Just above the reservoir, crystal clear waters flowed from a spring. As it ran downhill, they could see where some of it had been diverted to the reservoir for treatment. They looked across the waters and spotted a wooden barricade that held back the waters. When opened, the waters would spill into the creeks infecting the entire island's water supply.

Below the reservoir, they could see the huge smoldering fires that created the haze covering the lowlands of the island. As they watched, they saw other enforcers throwing harvested branches and various plants into the pit, obviously on a regular schedule.

With this new information, both men made a renewed effort to quickly return to Azriel and the other men so they could establish their plan of action. Time to act was running out!

It was nearly nightfall before Keoni and Gabor returned. Though still in a sweat from the uphill climb, Keoni was eager to report what they had found as Azriel and his team gathered around.

"We discovered what appears to an old trail along the edge of the plateau that leads down to the reservoir, but the pathway is quite narrow and treacherous at times."

"While we were near the reservoir, we overheard two men discussing their plan for releasing the infected waters,"

Keoni informed him. "It looks like sometime tomorrow, once their final testing is complete, the gates will be opened. We also took note of their fire pit location."

"Yes," Azriel replied. "I have been studying that fire pit from up here. I think there will be some changes to their plans once we get there."

Soberly, the twelve trained warriors nodded in anticipation for this upcoming assault. This is what they had prepared for. Though unsure about what lay before them, they knew if they did not succeed, many lives in the lowlands would be lost or at the very least, enslaved to an angry, power-crazed man with no regard for any life other than his own.

Quietly, Azriel placed his hand out in front of his companions. One by one, they each placed their hand on top of his. Once this was done, Azriel looked at his faithful friends and skilled warriors and spoke with authority.

"For Elemet, Chen, and the residents of Kumani!"

"So be it!" the men replied in low tones.

"Tomorrow, some will take to the air. Some will move through the trees, but all of us will be led by the instructions of Elemet to eventually see every captive set free from that which enslaves," Azriel reminded them. "Let us all retire to our tents to prepare for the important day before us."

As the men slowly moved towards their own tents, Azriel motioned for Keoni and Gabor to join him off to the side so they could eat and be refreshed while describing all the details of their journey. As he listened, Azriel felt a growing concern for the timing of all that needed to happen.

"We don't know the exact time of their final testing of the waters, correct?" Azriel asked.

"No, we don't," Keoni confirmed.

"We need to get to that reservoir right after that final testing is done so they will be completely unaware of any changes," Azriel stated. "I know this has been a long day of traveling for both of you, but since you are the only ones who know exactly where to go, I am asking if you are willing to make a return journey tomorrow. Do you think you can do that?"

Keoni and Gabor looked at each other for a moment before Gabor responded.

"Absolutely."

"Once you are in position, I need you to watch for that final testing before you pour this antidote into the waters." Azriel pulled a small glass vial from his clothing, and handing it to Keoni. "Guard this with your life. It is a gift from Chen and our only hope to purify the waters again."

"We will," Keoni replied soberly.

"Once the waters have been taken care of, we will wait for your signal to take to the skies on the backs of the eagles to finish what we've been called to do. I have seen a clearing on the other side of Camp Coshek where your eagles can pick you up."

"And how shall we signal you?" Keoni inquired.

Again, Azriel reached into his clothing and pulled out a small ram's horn which he placed into Gabor's hands.

"Once the horn has been blown, run as quickly as you can to the clearing," he instructed them. "The eagles flying overhead will hopefully distract the enforcers, giving you a chance to take to the air. Does this sound acceptable?"

"Yes, we can do this," Keoni replied.

"Thank you, my friends," Azriel answered. "Once you have eaten your fill, go and rest because tomorrow we have an early start."

Before he retired, Azriel stood and hugged these brave men so willing to endanger their own lives for the rescue of others. As he left, his own mind was spinning in nervousness. Yes, he himself was willing to lay down his life for others, but how could he possibly ask his companions to do the same?

As he approached his tent, Azriel heard a familiar voice that set all his fears at ease.

"It is not you asking these men to risk their lives. I am the one asking." he said.

Azriel's heart pounded as he entered into his private domain. Light flooded his tent as Elemet himself ministered to the man, preparing him for what lay ahead.

Chapter Twenty-Three

TRACKING THE TYRANT

Waning daylight would normally have been an issue for Mendi as he moved along the trail towards a region he had never visited before. Tension mounted in his back and neck muscles as he moved ahead in stealth mode. Confidently he followed the light before him, but the idea of meeting one of Hamah's drug-induced enforcers was not something he relished.

Mendi reminded himself that he was not alone in this endeavor. He had an unfair advantage in scouting out Hamah's whereabouts because Elemet was fully aware of Hamah's location. All he had to do was follow the light and listen for any further instructions. Though following Elemet was rather new, the instructions he received from Miss Haddie at the home of her sister, Ms. Bina, had been clear and concise.

As he walked, his mind wandered back to sweet Yona. There was something about her that drew him to her. She was a beauty, but beyond that, she showed great strength of character and tenacity in resisting Zelig's plans to marry her. He respected her greatly, though she was only twelve years old. He felt as though it was his destiny to stand up and help protect this child-woman from the domination of Cobar and other village elders like him.

Recalling his last moments with both Yona and Ms. Bina, he suddenly remembered the return of the old woman's eyesight after years of blindness. "Wow!" he thought to himself. "That was an interesting turn of events." He only hoped that when people came around, Ms. Bina would remember to continue acting as though she was still blind.

"Step behind a tree now!" he heard a voice instruct him. Mendi was startled to hear the voice so clearly, but still managed to follow through with its directives. He quickly moved behind a large tree on his side, sliding downward to assure he was completely hidden from sight. As he sat on the ground, he heard the crunch of the dry leaves scattered across the path. He held his breath as the person walked by.

Peering through the brush near the base of the tree, he saw the backside of a man as he passed his location. The man appeared to be looking for someone as he carefully scouted the woods for any sign of movement. Once satisfied that all was clear, he retraced his steps back in the direction he had come from.

Mendi's heart pounded as he waited in silence for the man to pass by. Once he was certain there was no other movement around him, he stood up and timidly peered onto the trail he had been following. Unsure if he should continue walking or move through the foliage, he waited another few moments for further instructions.

Suddenly the light reappeared before him and seemed to indicate it was time for him to leave the regularly traveled trail and take a less traveled path leading through the trees. This was not his favorite thing to do, but he realized he must be getting closer to Hamah's secret location. He wisely decided that venturing through the woods would be a much more secure way for him to move ahead. He just needed to learn the exact location of Hamah and report this information back to Cobar.

"Hamah does not know who you are. You have nothing to fear," the voice instructed him. "Enter the village to seek lodging for the night."

Mendi decided to follow the light which directed him to an alternate entrance into the village and thus avoid drawing attention to himself. Night was rapidly falling as he walked through the darkening forest trying desperately not to give into the fears of his past.

Just about the time he felt as though his confidence might fail, he was directed to step into a clearing where a young girl was drawing water from a well. Startled by his appearance, the girl looked up to see who it was.

"Hi," Mendi greeted her. "I didn't mean to startle you. I must have overlooked the main trail on my journey and ended up here. Can you tell me where I am?"

"This is the village of Elkin," she replied timidly.

"Can you tell me where I might find a place to sleep for the night?" he continued.

"We do have an inn near the marketplace, but things have been pretty busy since those strangers came."

"Oh, dear. I really do need a place to sleep this evening."

"Well," the girl responded, "we do have a room in our barn, but I will have to check with my mother to see if it's alright."

"That would be great," he replied with a smile. "My name is Mendi," he said while extending his hand.

The bronzed-skinned child quickly returned his smile as she shook his hand. She liked him. Though only eight years old, the young girl was wise beyond her years. She had been present when her father, accused as a dissenter, had been handcuffed and led away. Her mother watched helplessly as her sweet husband was taken, but rather than giving over to fear and self-pity, Lahela had seen her mother rise up and take the lead in providing for them. Her mother's courage in the face of loss inspired her.

"My name is Lahela," she volunteered even as her dark eyes studied Mendi's wavy chestnut hair. She noticed a slight glow about him that lingered even as the forest behind him grew darker. This puzzled her.

"Nice to meet you, Lahela," Mendi answered. "I will wait right here until I hear what your mother thinks. Okay?"

"Okay." Lahela picked up her water jugs and hurried off to find her mother. In a rather short period of time, the girl returned with her mother in tow. Mendi could immediately sense her self-confidence, making him feel a little uncomfortable at first. Recalling the real purpose of his journey, he took a breath while facing down his own discomfort.

"Mother, this is the man I was telling you about," she said with a smile. "His name is Mendi."

After quickly sizing up the stranger, the woman decided that he appeared safe enough. "Hi Mendi," she said. "Lahela seems to have made a new friend. My name is Pacey. I hear you are looking for lodging for the night. Is that right?"

"Yes, I got sidetracked off the main trail and ended up here," he explained. "Lahela told me that you might have a room where I could stay for the night."

"I suppose you could call it a room. It is actually in the loft above the barn where we keep our goats," she replied. "I can't promise it smells very pleasant either. I would normally refer you to our inn near the village square, however, with all the recent visitors we've had lately, I'm afraid the inn is probably full right now. Our loft is all I have to offer you."

"Lahela did mention that to me earlier," Mendi commented. "The loft would be just fine for tonight. I will be on my way tomorrow."

"Actually, I would enjoy some company, even if it was for only one night. Adult conversation doesn't occur very often around here, especially since my husband was arrested last year."

Lahela, overhearing her mother's comment, was a little annoyed. "I talk with you!"

"Yes, Lahela," she responded, "but there are some things I can only discuss with other adults."

"Like what?" Lahela pressed her.

"Like when it is time for a child to allow her mother some time for grown-up conversation," she answered with a stern look that meant it was time for her daughter to hold her peace.

"Hmm," the girl mused, obviously not impressed with her mother's answer. The child spun around, and headed back towards their cabin.

"I'm sorry," she said while turning back to Mendi. "Lahela isn't used to sharing my attention."

"Not a problem. May I ask what your husband was arrested for?"

"He was accused of being a dissenter, but all he did was question the village elders' decisions on some things. He wasn't trying to cause any problems, but they just didn't like being questioned on anything. He was arrested shortly after that."

"I'm sorry," Mendi replied.

"I hope staying with us won't cause you any danger," Pacey commented. "It is getting dark, so you should be relatively safe for tonight. The only threat might be if one of my neighbors come by in the morning to purchase some cheese or milk."

"I'm not worried. I've seen and heard enough to realize that it's too late for me to be controlled by fear."

"Well, then Mendi, you are welcome to join us. Have you had supper yet?"

"Actually, I haven't eaten for a while. Supper would be wonderful! Thank you."

"This way to our home," she directed him.

As they walked from the well towards her cabin, Mendi couldn't help but notice something very different about this striking woman. Her darkened skin let him know she wasn't afraid to work and actually, she didn't seem much afraid of anything as she led the way back. Last year's arrest of her husband didn't slow her down in any way. He wondered if she knew something more than what she was saying.

He cringed as he thought back to how he had once assisted the village elders as they gathered information on those opposing them and then abruptly had them arrested. Things had certainly changed for him personally. Now instead of trying to please those he was working for without regard of how this affected others, he was hunting down the newest and most deadly of tyrants. Though he had switched his allegiance to Elemet and those following the way of the eagle, that had to remain a secret for the time being.

Meanwhile, Pacey was having some concerns of her own. Though she sensed Mendi was not a threat, she didn't want her "other activities" to be exposed either. Much preparation had gone into their plans and she could not risk failing at this point. Consequently, both of them walked silently, obviously deep in thought.

Chapter Twenty-Four

STEPPING INTO DESTINY

The howl of wolves filled the night air as Shoshanna nervously moved through the darkened forest. Thorny branches grabbed at her clothing, causing her sleeves and skirt to rip as she pushed her way forward. The scratches on her arms stung as she strove to protect her face from the bramble all around. Her progression towards the dim light she could barely see was slow and difficult. Suddenly, she could hear snarling wolves directly behind her.

Panic set in.

She thrashed at the branches and thorns trying to keep her from the light she sought. The deep-throated growls let her know the wolves were nearly upon her and she had no defense. Quickly, she remembered what she had seen Galen do when the enforcers appeared while they traveled through the smoking mountains.

"Elemet!"

Instantly, Shoshanna was surrounded by light as she opened her eyes. The terrifying dream had vanished and once again peace washed over her. Elemet's presence was very real and as she continued lying in her bed, she could hear his voice clearer than she ever had before.

"Guard your thoughts, my child," he advised her.

"But how can I do that if I am sleeping?" she asked.

"What were you thinking about before you went to bed?" he prodded her.

A recollection of all she had been thinking about rushed into her mind. She was nervous about their return to the lowlands scheduled for today. Images of the angry mob of enforcers rushing upon her and her companions before their escape into the woods had created a traumatic memory in her soul. The fear of that moment was still very fresh in her mind, though it had occurred many months back.

"The fear needs to be loosed from your soul so that when you return to the lowlands, that memory will not plague you," Elemet explained. "All things have become new in you, however, your soul and the memories it carries must be cleansed in cooperation with your own will."

"And how do I do that?" Shoshanna asked, even more perplexed than before.

"Say out loud what I show you," he responded.

Immediately smoky, translucent letters appeared, creating words and sentences. Reading what was before her, Shoshanna said, "By my own choice and as an act of my will, I loose fear, worry, traumatic memories, unbelief, and all things contrary to the way of the eagle from my soul. I bind to my soul trust in Elemet, peace in Chen, and confidence in the light that directs my way."

As soon as she had finished reading the wispy words before her, they vanished.

At once, the lingering trauma from the darkness vanished, much like the dawning sunlight that entered the room through her window. Her lungs breathed in the peace that now surrounded her, refreshing her body, soul, and spirit with renewed confidence and hope.

Today was the day she, Galen, and Roany would join the hundreds who had already gone before them to their assigned destinations. Though anxious to begin their own assignments, a twinge of nervousness still remained as she didn't know what they would face upon their arrival.

Dressing quickly, Shoshanna left her room at the Ashlene Lodge for it was nearly time to join her two companions. As she stepped out the front door, she recalled hearing another resident calling the lodge a place of dreams and encounters. With the instructions from Elemet fresh in her mind, she hastened her pace to the Hub. The same archway that Uri had stepped through previously, now awaited them.

Strange. She had not yet seen Galen and Roany. Usually, both young men met her in front of the lodge each day. Wondering if she had missed her friends completely, she imagined them already standing next to the portal, awaiting her arrival. As she rushed up the stairs to the front doors, she looked up and was surprised to see Chen standing in front of her.

"Good morning, Shoshanna," he greeted her. "I've been expecting you."

"You were?" she answered in surprise.

"Yes, come join me. We have some things we need to discuss before I send you back to the lowlands."

"Shouldn't Galen and Roany be here as well?"

"They will be here," Chen assured her, "but their departures will be after your own. You each have your own assignments to fulfill before the final segment of your journey and your task is especially dear to my heart."

Shoshanna was listening, but the thought of not having her friends at her side, especially Galen, brought her a moment of panic. She had grown quite attached to their companionship and counsel during their journeys together.

Fully aware of her misgivings, Chen spoke. "Did you not travel alone when you first learned the way of the eagle?" he reminded her.

"Yes. That is true," she admitted.

"Were you afraid when Miss Haddie sent you out?"

In an instant, the memories of all she had done prior to her trip through the smoking mountains returned. Yes, she traveled the trails of the forest many times on her own, especially during her training with Miss Haddie and then when she had been sent out on assignments. She recalled how she had once delivered a meal to Galen and Uri when they were held in prison. She had also delivered a pie and some of Miss Haddie's sweet tea, along with a word of encouragement to Galen's parents. She felt a new confidence rise up in her again. Yes, the light had always led her safely to wherever she needed to go.

"No, I wasn't afraid," she responded. "In fact, I asked Miss Haddie to send me, especially since I had first failed to follow her directions exactly." Her eyes dropped as she recalled the moment of first discovering the consequences of her blunder, but Chen was quick to reply.

"And yet, in spite of your mistake, Galen's arrest helped Roany decide who he was going to listen to. When Roany heard of Galen and Uri's escape from prison, he left his village to join them. You see, when you admitted your mistake, Elemet was able to impact and redeem others as he turned things around for the good of everyone. Even the mistakes you and your friends made while traveling through the smoking mountains resulted in many valuable lessons for each of you. Can you see that now?"

"Yes, I can see that," she acknowledged. "Is this the way it always is? We make mistakes and Elemet uses them for our benefit?"

"It can be like that for a time, if people are quick to humble themselves and admit their failures. But, the ultimate goal is to see everyone cast out the fear and lies so they can clearly hear instructions and follow the light of Elemet without deviation. That is when life will be very different here on the island of Kumani. Do you understand?" he asked, gazing deeply into her eyes with love.

Waves of courage and renewed passion flooded Shoshanna as she stared into the pools of eternity found in his eyes. All the self-doubt fled in his presence as she was reminded of what she had learned these past months.

In a moment of time, Shoshanna knew that whatever Chen asked of her, she would be willing to do.

"So what is it that you would have me attend to? I am willing to go wherever you send me," she responded with a smile.

Greatly pleased with her change of heart, Chen explained Shoshanna's assignment to her.

"Near the village of Kieran, there is a cave hidden from sight where some families have taken refuge from the fires of destruction, the onslaught of the enforcers, the haze, and the tainted waters to be released from Camp Coshek. Some of them have already become sick. Some are injured, and all of them, including the children, are scared. They have run out of food."

"What can I do for them?" Shoshanna asked, feeling bewildered by their difficult circumstances.

"I am sending you as my emissary to bring comfort and hope to them as you lead them to safety."

"And where am I leading them?"

"You are leading them to my house of refuge where they will be safe until all this trauma is over," Chen explained. "Their fear of men is great at this time, so that is why I am sending you. I want you to bring healing to them and also provide the food they will need during the journey."

Puzzled by his request, Shoshanna had another question.

"How am I to heal them and feed them?"

"How did you minister healing to Uri when he fell? And, how did your group eat when you were traveling through the smoking mountains?"

"You provided everything for us," Shoshanna answered.

"You will also see the same provision for this journey as well," Chen responded. "As you follow the light, teach the refugees as they travel with you. They will learn the way of the eagle just as you did."

Shoshanna nodded in agreement with all Chen was asking of her, though it did feel quite overwhelming to be asked to do all this on her own. Chen started walking towards the archway leading to her new assignment, so Shoshanna followed him. He continued speaking as they moved closer to her moment of departure. She was listening, but was a little saddened that she would not be able to say good bye to her companions before she left, especially Galen.

Once they arrived at the archway, Chen turned toward her to release her final instructions. Noticing a slight smile come across his face, Shoshanna wondered if there was something he had not yet revealed.

"I am proud of your courage, my friend," he said. "Because of your willingness to go on this assignment alone, I am giving you a gift."

Her curiosity piqued, she had to ask, "And what is it?"

"I am sending some of my warriors with you. They will fight on your behalf as you have need of them."

Shoshanna's eyes grew wide in astonishment as the outline of translucent beings appeared before her. She counted twelve warriors now standing around her and Chen. The sight of these mighty soldiers left her stunned and without words. Chen continued.

"These warriors will always be at your beck and call, but understand that no one else will be able to see them. You will not always see them yourself, but they have been assigned to you and only you can send them out as you need. They will enter through the archway with you and will remain with you until they are no longer needed. The only battle you need to engage in is the one that occurs in your own mind. Do you recall the things Elemet spoke to you about this morning?"

"Yes. I must always reject any thoughts or memories contrary to the goodness of Elemet and the ways of the eagle, especially fear," she responded.

"And if the thoughts come into your mind to cause you fear?" Chen prodded her.

"I loose them from my soul, and bind to my soul trust in Elemet, peace in you, and confidence in the light that leads me. Right?"

"Good! Now you are ready," he encouraged her.

Just as Chen finished, Galen and Roany, obviously out of breath, came rushing up to the archway.

"Chen, Shoshanna! I am so glad to see you here. When we couldn't find you at the lodge, we became concerned that we were late for our sending off," Galen explained.

"No need for concern, my friends," Chen responded. "You have arrived at the perfect time to send Shoshanna off on her mission. Yours will be next."

"What?" Galen was stunned. "I thought we were all going together."

"You are all going," Chen assured him, "but not all together. You will meet again in the near future, but for now each of you must go as the light leads you. There is much that needs to be accomplished in the lowlands. All of you are ready and prepared. You may say good bye to Shoshanna for the time being, and then we will talk before you go to where you are the most needed."

Taking a moment to calm himself, Galen nodded towards Chen and then stepped up close to Shoshanna so they could speak privately. Grabbing her hand, he led her aside.

"I didn't think we would be going on separate missions," Galen admitted. "I've grown accustomed to being with you."

"I know," Shoshanna agreed. "It was hard for me to hear about the plan at first, but Chen has granted me everything I need to do this. I'm sure he will do the same for you."

A few seconds of silence hung in the air as they solemnly stared at each other. Shoshanna continued. "Chen says we will be together again at a later time, but for now..."

Galen interrupted. "Before we say good bye, I want to give you something so you will remember me." Reaching into the pocket of his shirt, Galen produced a small stone set in a golden ring. The dazzling stone itself seemed ablaze with flashing lights and colors emanating from it. The sight of it took Shoshanna's breath away.

"Oh Galen! Where did you find such a lovely stone?" she exclaimed in wonder.

"Do you remember our journey through that canyon before entering the Eagles' Nest?"

"Of course I do."

Galen proceeded. "When Uri was carrying you after you twisted your ankle, I happened to look down on the ground and found this stone just sitting there. I picked it up, had it made into a ring and was saving it for the perfect moment...and I guess this is it."

Taking a deep breath, Galen lifted up Shoshanna's hand and looked into her eyes once again.

"Shoshanna, would you honor me by wearing this ring as a reminder of my love for you? It is my hope and desire that when this is over, we might become husband and wife."

Tears formed in Shoshanna's eyes as she looked upon the man she had come to love and respect through all their journeys together. She carefully considered her words before speaking.

"I would be honored to wear this ring as a memorial of our friendship and our love. And when this is over, let us see what amazing things Elemet has planned for us."

Tenderly, Shoshanna allowed Galen to place the ring on her finger. As he did so, he glanced back at Chen. Chen smiled and nodded. With that, Galen gave Shoshanna a kiss on her cheek as the two embraced.

The embrace was lasting a little longer than Roany was comfortable with, so he spoke up.

"Okay, you two! There are others here who would also like to say goodbye, if you don't mind!"

Laughing, as tears ran down their faces, Galen and Shoshanna walked back to the group now gathering at the archway to watch as Shoshanna stepped into her destiny. After giving hugs to Roany and other friends, including Talia, the one Roany had been quite taken with, Shoshanna stepped up to Chen to say goodbye to him as well.

"You will take good care of Galen for me, right?"

"Of course I will," Chen responded. "And remember, you are never alone."

Glancing around at her twelve, translucent, and fierce-looking warriors standing at attention around her, she had to smile. "I think I will be fine. Thank you, Chen!" She gave Chen one final hug before stepping through the archway and vanishing from sight.

Chapter Twenty-Five

THE BEST LAID PLANS

igh in the mountains, the sun rose early, casting its brilliance everywhere. Even the sides of the twelve tents glistened as the bright rays reflected off the accumulated morning dew.

The day was calling.

Still groggy with sleep, he stretched, turning on his side. His sleep had been sweet and his dreams filled with breathtaking dives upon the back of his beloved eagle, Zuko. The refreshing rest had been so complete, he momentarily forgot where he was. Then he remembered his encounter with Elemet the night before and his eyes burst open.

Now it all came back to him. Today was the day he and his men had trained many months for. They had drilled and rehearsed leaping from the backs of these great birds and rolling on the ground to break their falls. They had even planned quick retrievals, should it become necessary to rescue one of their team. Even though they had done all they knew to do, Azriel was fully aware that Elemet would give them directives during the battle. Their lives depended on how quickly they each responded.

Though Azriel and his men were hopeful that they would return victorious, they also knew that Camp Coshek was the noose Hamah had secretly prepared to take over Kumani. Without their assistance, many innocent people would either die or succumb to the mind-numbing effects of both the haze and the tainted drinking water. Each man had willingly made the decision to either fully succeed in their mission or die trying. Azriel had also made the decision to do everything within his power to protect the lives of these friends he had come to love so they could all return to their homes and families.

With the wisdom and counsel of Elemet still clear in his mind, Azriel arose and pulled back the flap of his tent. It was time for action.

After quickly rousing his men, he was pleased to discover that both Keoni and Gabor had already begun their descent to the reservoir and would be certain to arrive at their destination shortly. As he scanned the skies around him, he noticed a gathering of their eagles on a distant tree not too far from their location. The eagles would be arriving soon, so he instructed his men to tear down the camp, gather their supplies, and prepare to mount their eagles for battle.

As they completed their final preparations, he could hear the words of Elemet ringing in his ears. "Remember, the enforcers you now battle were once dissenters who longed for freedom. They also have families and loved ones who miss them dearly. You must succeed in destroying Hamah's plans, but remember, these men were robbed of their free will. There may yet be hope for their restoration."

Peering over the side of the overhang, Azriel studied the edge of the reservoir, looking signs of his companions. As he watched, he saw ten or so enforcers beginning to gather. He knew they would be tending the smoldering fires and testing the toxic waters. Hoping his men were in position, Azriel decided to signal the eagles by grabbing the mirror he had and directing the rays of the sun towards the perching eagles. Immediately, all twelve of the birds launched into the air, heading towards their location.

Once again, he looked to the right side of the reservoir; he noticed some movement in the bushes. Thankfully, he took a breath of relief. It appeared as if Keoni and Gabor had taken up their positions.

The timing had to be perfect to accomplish their two objectives. So much depended on it!

The enforcers below split up, each heading for their designated assignments that day. Eight of the men moved towards the fire pit. Several of them carried containers to be added to the flames. The rest went to gather wood to add to the fire. The winds blowing down from the mountains forced the toxic fumes into the lowlands. Two enforcers headed towards the reservoir to proceed with the final testing before the infected waters were to be released.

While the enforcers took care of their duties, the aerial warriors mounted the eagles in preparation for their onslaught. Their hope was to distract the enemies, allowing Keoni and Gabor to safely make it across the grounds of

Camp Coshek. At the clearing on the far side of the camp, they could mount their own eagles and fly off unharmed—at least that was the plan.

Nervously, they awaited the sound of the ram's horn, announcing the beginning of the attack. Even the eagles could feel the tension and had to be calmed down by their riders. Finally, Azriel could wait no longer. Dismounting his eagle, he motioned for the other men and their birds to remain in position while he checked the bushes where Keoni and Gabor should be waiting.

The two enforcers had already completed final testing of the waters and appeared to be heading towards the release gate.

"Where are they?" he wondered silently, while studying the side of the reservoir one more time. "Could they have had a mishap of some sort?"

All of a sudden, Keoni emerged from the bushes and quickly poured out the contents of the vial Chen had given them and slipped back undercover of the vegetation.

Greatly relieved, Azriel quickly returned to his mount, just as they heard the ram's horn sounding in the air. At once, the eagles spread their wings and lifted in the air above Camp Coshek. One rider and his eagle pushed the beam holding back the boulders they had piled up on the edge of the ridge and watched as the boulders bounced down the cliff towards the reservoir.

The eagles squawked and squealed in excitement as they and their riders dropped a barrage of rocks upon the enforcers below, sending them scattering. The boulders splashed into the reservoir, causing some of the waters to overflow its banks in the direction of the smoldering fire pit just below. The rocks continued steadily, especially focusing on the southern rim in hopes of creating a breech in the levy so all the waters would flow directly into the pit, quenching the fires completely.

However, the enforcers returned with something the warriors had not counted on. Crossbows! It was obvious the enforcers had been trained to defend the camp from any type of assault.

As the arrows flew around them, Azriel and his men were forced to press even tighter against the bodies of the eagles, allowing them to perform aerial maneuvers avoiding the arrows and so they could continue their own bombardment of stones, now focusing on the weapons used against them.

In the midst of the chaos below, Azriel noticed his two men carefully moving past warring enforcers, donning blue shirts looking exactly like those the enforcers were wearing. Chen had been so wise in providing for his warriors in every way. Their movements across the compound had not yet been noticed. For that he was thankful.

Circling far above, he noticed the levy was still holding. Observing one large beam holding up the final release of the waters, Azriel spoke calmly to his eagle, Zuko, describing the necessary maneuver needed to free the waters. Zuko seemed to understand and began his rapid dive towards the log with Azriel hanging on as best he could.

Arrows were still flying around them, as the two of them approached the waters. Suddenly Zuko turned upward with talons extended towards the log. The impact of their contact caused Azriel to lose his seating and tumble into the reservoir. Zuko managed to successfully dislodge the log. The waters poured out towards the fire pit.

The upsurge of waters flooded everywhere, sending the enforcers running in all directions trying to get out of the way its pathway. Destruction was seen everywhere.

Horrified, the team realized Azriel was no longer with them.

Keoni and Gabor had made it to the clearing and successfully mounted their own eagles. Though they circled above several times, no one could see any sign of Azriel. They wondered if the waters had somehow washed him into the fire pit. Even Zuko seemed greatly distraught by the loss of his rider.

Eventually, Keoni made the difficult decision for them to return to the Eagles' Nest without Azriel. Soberly, the eleven men made their journey back to report both their success, as well as the devastating loss of Azriel.

Chapter Twenty-Six

SECRETS AND SURPRISES

"**M**s. Bina, more people have arrived looking for help," Yona said, a little exasperated with all the houseguests already filling up much of the space in their expanding cabin. "Where are we going to put them all?"

"No worries, child," Ms. Bina responded, while getting out of her bed. The early morning visitors were becoming a regular occurrence now. "I'm certain Oren will be arriving shortly to escort them to the house of refuge, just like the others before them. The truth is getting out and that is good. These dear people have no idea where to go. Let them come in to join us. We can always make room for more. Now that I can see again, I can help as well."

"Yes, but remember Mendi wanted you to keep your restored vision undercover for a while. I still think that is good idea," Yona added. "The only thing I wonder about is whether or not there might be some informants, secretly posing as dissenters among those coming to us. That concerns me sometimes."

"That is something that I am able to help with also," Ms. Bina responded with a smile. "Elemet has gifted me with the ability to recognize those genuinely looking for help, and those with hidden motives. If I see anyone here who does not belong, I will certainly speak up."

"Yes, however, what are we to do if they have already come inside?"

"Yona, don't allow fear or worry to rob your peace and joy. You must remember Elemet is fully able to guard this house and the people needing our help. He is the one orchestrating this plan, so we need to simply rest in his wisdom and guidance."

Realizing that Ms. Bina was absolutely right, Yona took a deep breath releasing all her worries and concerns to the only one capable of carrying it all. Immediately, her peace returned. As Ms. Bina dressed, preparing to greet their new guests, Yona returned to the back door to invite their new guests inside. She quickly scanned outside to see if there was any sign of Oren. Seeing no one, she closed the back door and focused her attention on this latest group of people settling in.

Shortly, Ms. Bina exited her bedroom and walked down the hallway towards her living room, now filled with men, women, and a few children, hoping to find their way of escape out from under the control of the village elders. Word was spreading quickly as the tea party movement gave hope to those opening themselves up to the truth.

On the opposite side of the village, another meeting was also occurring in a back room of the print shop.

"All the village elders have been notified of our secret meeting, Father," Zelig confidently informed Cobar.

"And, are you certain Hamah does not know about it?"

"Well, all the village elders I met with are terrified of Hamah and were anxious to see him taken care of. They had heard about the burning of Yashen and wanted to make sure their villages are not next on his list of extermination. I am certain that none of them would be sharing tomorrow night's plans for our secret gathering."

"That's good! Did you see any sign of his enforcers while you were traveling?" Cobar asked in concern.

"Not that I noticed, anyway."

"I have yet to hear back from Mendi regarding Hamah's actual location, but I really was not counting on him returning that quickly. Hamah only gave me one week to inform the elders of his 'operating changes.' I just hope we can pull this off before Hamah releases the next influx of toxins into the waters of Kumani. We need to quickly get our own enforcers up to Camp Coshek as soon as possible so we can find out what is going on up there."

"This will be discussed tomorrow night, right?"

"Yes. That and much more. Okay, so I need you to get up to the front office now so we can still maintain our business operations as normally as possible," Cobar stated.

"Oh, by the way," Zelig added. "I did notice quite a number of villagers traveling on the trails throughout the forests. I'm not sure what that is about."

"Well, it's not something to worry us right now. Our first concern is 'Lord' Hamah," he added with a mocking scorn to the title Hamah had given himself.

Nodding, Zelig went up to the front desk to see if anyone might come in while Cobar continued finalizing his plans for the downfall of Hamah and his enforcers.

Though laying only on straw with rough blankets serving as his bedding, Mendi slept peacefully through the night. However, at first daylight, he quickly remembered where he was. Instead of the comfortable inns he was accustomed to, Mendi awoke to a commotion of hungry goats, bleating loudly on the floor of the barn beneath him. Shortly after the feeding, he heard the creaking of the ladder leading to the opening of the loft where he had slept.

Brown curls appeared first, followed by Lahela's beaming face as she peeked into the loft. Seeing that Mendi was already awake, the girl greeted their guest.

"Mother told me not to bother you, but I thought I would check and see if you were awake yet."

"Oh yes. I'm awake now."

"Good! I've been up for a while. I've even fed the goats," she added proudly. "Did you like our loft? This is one of my favorite places to hang out whenever we don't have guests, of course."

"Yes, the loft is quite nice," Mendi responded, even though his nose quickly reminded him that animals were living just below.

"Mother is just starting breakfast right now, but I was wondering if I could show you my secret hideout before we eat. It's not too far away. You want to come with me?"

Seeing Lahela's hopeful eyes, Mendi knew he could not turn down her offer without offending the child. "I would love to see your secret hideout, however, wouldn't your mother want to know if we left the homestead right now?"

"Oh! Okay, I'll just tell her we are going so she won't worry," the child decided. "I'll be right back." The girl disappeared giving Mendi a few minutes to really wake up and gather his thoughts before she returned.

He got up and brushed off the particles of hay still clinging to his clothing. Gathering his few belongings, Mendi put them back in his knapsack and took one quick sip of water from the gourd he carried before the child returned.

"Mother says it is fine and that breakfast will be ready when we return," Lahela informed him.

"Well then, I guess we should be off on our adventure," he said with a smile. "You lead the way and I'll follow."

Thrilled, Lahela quickly scaled the ladder and headed out the barn door with Mendi in close pursuit. The two of them weaved through the forest on a trail that Mendi could see had been used quite often by this ambitious child. She scampered like a cat in, around, and through openings that Mendi would not have chosen on his own, but his curiosity to see where this led pressed him onward.

Finally, after what seemed an eternity to the man, Lahela came to a stop, motioning for Mendi to join her in the hollowed out area surrounded by thick bushes. A small dirty blanket covered the ground with two small tree stumps serving as chairs for the child's hideout.

As he crawled in on hands and knees, he could see why Lahela loved her little hideaway. With the foliage so dense, she could easily sit there without ever being noticed by anyone. Mendi respectfully took his seat next to her. The child showed him how she was able to part some of the leaves and look out upon the activities of the village of Elkin.

While observing the new visitors to the inn that Lahela had spoken of, Mendi noticed that two of the enforcers were standing close enough for him to hear what they were saying. Looking towards the child, he held up one finger to his lips, indicating they needed to be very quiet as they listened.

"Lord Hamah has just received word that there is to be a secret meeting of the village elders tomorrow night," the first man stated. "He wants you to notify all available enforcers, instructing them to join him at the gathering place so we can fulfill his plans for that evening."

"I understand," the second man replied. "I'll send out the messengers immediately." As the two men parted ways, Mendi could feel the tension building in him. Lahela looked puzzled as to why he seemed so concerned about this conversation.

Once it was safe, Mendi encouraged the girl to lead the way back home before they spoke. Shortly, the two of them reappeared at the homestead, but instead of smiling, Mendi's brow was now furrowed in concern as Lahela led him into the kitchen.

Opening the door, they were welcomed with the scent of fried potatoes, sweet rolls, and scrambled eggs, reminding them of how hungry they were. Pacey turned to greet the adventurers, but quickly noticed something was troubling Mendi. Looking towards Lahela, she questioned her daughter.

"What has happened?"

Innocently, Lahela explained, "I just took him to see my hideout like I told you, but while we were there, we heard some men talking."

"And, what did they say?" she asked Mendi, realizing he could better explain the situation.

"They spoke of some plans made by a very dangerous man, now staying at the inn," Mendi replied. "I was sent here to discover his whereabouts, but now I fear things are moving too quickly for me to report back to my employer."

Now Pacey became concerned. "And who is your employer?"

"Well, actually there is one man to whom I pose as an employee, but my true allegiance is to another."

"It is important for me to know where your true allegiance lies and who this dangerous man is," Pacey stated as she stood her ground. "How you respond will decide whether you may stay or whether I ask you to leave immediately."

Clearing his throat, Mendi knew he needed to reveal more about himself than he ever intended. "My true allegiance is to Elemet and the way of the eagle. I am only posing as an informant to a village elder in order to gain further information on what is being planned."

"And, how do I know with certainty that you are not an informant for a village elder?"

"You have every right to ask that," Mendi admitted. "The truth is, not that long ago, I was operating as a true informant for the village elders, but I have had some encounters that have forever changed me. I could never go back to that old way of life. If you wouldn't mind giving me some time, I would love to explain who I've become."

Seeing the passion and sincerity in his eyes, Pacey agreed to listen to Mendi's story while they ate breakfast. Mendi started at the beginning, giving a brief account of all he had been through. Though careful not to mention any names, he described his encounters, and especially how he came to know Elemet.

When he had finished, he could see that both Pacey and Lahela had been greatly touched by his journey. Quickly Pacey began putting things together.

"So you are telling me that the two men you overheard outside the inn work for that dangerous man you mentioned earlier. Is that true?"

"Yes," he admitted. "The enforcers referred to him as Lord Hamah."

Pacey was silent for a moment, considering some things before she responded.

"I believe we are working on the same side," she said. "Though I have yet to meet Elemet as you described, I have come to recognize that the control the elders held over our villages is not for our good and survival as they propose. I attended a tea party at a neighboring village and learned the truth about the things we have been taught." Pacey continued:

"My husband recognized these things early on, and when he questioned the authority of the village elders, he was arrested as a dissenter. I have not seen him since that time, however, I decided that if he had the courage to challenge the elders, I would do my part to help others escape the control they have had over us."

"Yes, we help them!" Lahela added, unable to hold her peace any longer.

"We help hide them," Pacey added, "until a man named Oren comes to lead them to a safe place. It makes me nervous to hear that such a dangerous man is in our village right now."

"Well, the good news is that he will be leaving shortly," Mendi replied. "However, I do feel an urgency to go now so I can warn my friends of Hamah's plans. Though I have not yet met this man, Oren, I understand his skill is amazing. If he is the one helping you with those traveling through, you are in great hands.

"Thank you so much for allowing me to sleep here and providing a wonderful meal, but I do need to be on my way. When you see Oren next, please extend my greetings to him."

With that, Mendi stood to leave, but Pacey had one more request for him.

"As I told you, my husband was arrested and taken away. I don't know what has become of him, but I have a hope that someday he might return to us." With tears in her eyes, she continued. "In all your travels, if you ever come across a man named Jovan, please let him know that Lahela and I are still waiting for his return."

"If I meet him somewhere, I will let him know," Mendi answered, as he headed towards the door. "I do want to encourage you to call upon Elemet for yourself, that you might have the help you need to complete all that you have put your hand to."

"Thank you," Pacey said as she walked him to the door.

"And thank you for going with me to my hideout," Lahela added.

"You are very welcome," he answered. "And you are a brave girl to help your mom with everything she is doing."

"Thank you."

Mendi headed towards the woods while looking for the familiar light to direct him. Before he left the homestead, he turned once more to wave goodbye to his new friends.

Chapter Twenty-Seven

A NEW NORMAL

Once Shoshanna stepped through the archway, she was relieved to see both she and her entourage arrived safely in the lowlands. Though the haze was still present, she noticed that it was beginning to wane a little making the air easier to breath. That was a relief.

Taking a glance at the translucent warriors gathered around her, she decided she needed to learn more about this new resource she had been given. Shoshanna took a good look at the warriors dressed in gleaming armor over a white tunic. They carried no weapons, but the fierceness of their countenance indicated clearly that they were the weapons. Reminding herself that they were under her charge, she decided to address the one closest to her.

"So, what do I call you and how do I use your services here in the lowlands?"

The warrior bowed slightly before replying.

"My name is Eran and I am part of the host used to protect and defend the citizens of Kumani," he replied respectfully. "As the lead warrior for this troop, you can address me, and I will see to it that whenever you need protection, you are taken care of."

"Thank you, Eran," she replied. "And no one else can see you except for me?"

"Yes, that is true, however, if the need arises, we will not hesitate in showing ourselves to those threatening you."

"Well, that's good to know," she admitted. "So, what is the best way for me to use your services?"

"Ma'am, you may call for our assistance any time and we will be there. You may also send us out ahead before you go to make sure your path is clear. Then you can avoid any dangers along the way."

"So do I ask for your help or just call out when a crisis arises?"

"You command us. We will do as you direct to protect you. Any directions on where to go or what to do must come from the light that leads you. Chen or Elemet may also speak directly to you."

Nodding, Shoshanna realized that she would need to focus on the directions given to her along the way. She could not allow her ability to see the warriors cause a distraction to her purpose. It had been a little while since that kind of direction was needed, but it all came back to her quickly.

"Ok, I suppose we should be moving ahead now. I need to find those children and their families Chen spoke of." Noticing that the host were not conversing with her, Shoshanna decided she best focus on her task.

Her first thought was to locate the light directing her where to go. Looking to her right, she noticed the familiar light and started moving towards it. As she took a few steps, the host followed her every move. This was very distracting!

"Look Eran," Shoshanna said, "since I am not able to converse with you and your men, would you mind making yourselves less visible so I can pay better attention to my assignment?"

"Certainly, ma'am," he responded. Immediately he and the other warriors became almost invisible with only the barest of an outline showing their presence.

"That's better. Thank you. And since I am now moving ahead on the trail, I want to send some warriors ahead and some of you behind me to clear the way. If you see anything disturbing, please let me know."

"Yes, ma'am." The twelve warriors split into two groups and headed in different directions.

Taking a breath of relief, Shoshanna moved along the trail before her as directed by the light. Knowing that there was nothing to fear did give her a great sense of peace. She was very grateful that Chen had sent the host to help her.

The young woman ducked under some of the extended branches and pushed past the overgrown weeds on either side of the path as they grabbed at her clothing in resistance. In frustration, she noticed glimpses of the warriors easily passing through the brush, unhindered. She wondered if something could be done to speed up her progress. Her first thought was to ask Eran about it.

"Eran," she called out. "I have a question for you."

In seconds, he stood before her, waiting.

"Is there anything you can do to make this trail easier for me to pass through?" she asked.

Respectfully, Eran stated that their duty was only to protect her. If she needed other assistance, she should to speak to Elemet about it. Once he answered her question, he vanished to resume his duties.

Deciding that further assistance was required, Shoshanna made her appeal to Elemet, asking for his help. Shortly after she had finished talking, she decided to do her best to press through rough terrain. Suddenly, someone tapped her on the shoulder.

Thinking it was Eran wanting to report something, she turned around and was amazed to see Chen himself standing behind her.

"Chen! What are you doing here?" she exclaimed in amazement.

"You asked for some assistance. Right?"

"Well, yes. This trail is so overgrown, it is difficult for me to press through."

"Did you realize this is something you are already equipped to deal with?" he asked gently.

"I did ask Eran if he and his warriors could help me, but he made it clear their job was only to protect. What should I do about this?"

Smiling, Chen explained. "You speak to the trail and tell it to be made clear before you. Remember, you are now part of the family and whatever you have seen me do, you have that power and ability to do the same."

Shoshanna thought about this for a moment before responding.

"So I could speak to the trail and tell it to be made clear? Is that right?"

Chen was pleased with her grasp of what he was telling her. "You understand now. Think back on the many ways you have been moved here on Kumani. You have access to that at any time. If you see a doorway, you can step through it."

"And how do I see it?"

"You look for it expectantly and you will see it when you need it," he replied, "and the host will always go with you."

Shoshanna was beginning to understand.

Before Chen left, he informed Shoshanna of some important changes that she and the others needed to know.

"Azriel and his team were successful in destroying the source of the haze and the impending poisoning of the waters. Hamah and the village elders are unaware of these changes at the moment, but they will soon find out. I also want you to know that, unfortunately, Azriel did not return from his mission."

"What? Has he been lost?" she asked in a panic.

"I can tell you there is yet hope for his return, but many things must occur first."

"And what are those things?"

"That is not something for you to carry right now," Chen explained, "but you can make an appeal to Elemet regarding

Azriel's needed strength and the increased wisdom essential for him to overcome. That would be greatly appreciated."

"I will do that!" Shoshanna promised. "Can I tell the others about all this as well?"

"Yes, share with them all that you have learned."

"I will tell them."

"Good. Now I leave you to figure out how to use the resources and gifts for yourself. I am confident you can do this."

Once Chen finished, Shoshanna watched as he turned away, stepped into a cloud, and vanished before her.

"Wow!" she thought. "I wonder if that is something I could do at some time. Wouldn't that be amazing?"

While she processed this new information, Shoshanna turned back towards the overgrown trail she was to follow and thought about her options. But before she tackled her own challenges, she made her appeal to Elemet on behalf of Azriel. Wherever he was at that moment, she asked Elemet to flood him with renewed strength and sound wisdom to overcome his circumstances. When she was finished, a peace swept over her letting her know that Elemet had indeed heard her request and would respond appropriately.

"Now, to deal with this overgrowth!" she told herself.

Elsewhere on the island, Galen suddenly found himself in front of an unfamiliar cabin, located on the outskirts of the village of Chana. The light before him indicated he was to knock on the back door. Tension ran through his body as he approached the cabin and knocked. It had been a while since he had been in any of the villages.

A young woman answered the door, looking rather puzzled as she studied his face momentarily.

"I'm sorry to bother you, but I was sent here for some reason," he explained.

Suddenly it dawned on the young woman why his face seemed so familiar. "You're Galen!" she announced. "I am so honored to meet you. My name is Yona. I am good friends with Jessah."

"Yona! Yes, I remember Jessah telling us some of your experiences together. But how did you know who I am since we have never met?'

"Oh, I saw your picture posted in our village, 'warning' us about you 'dangerous' dissenters.

I told Jessah all about it when she last came to visit," Yona explained.

"Well, may I come in?" Galen asked, growing a little uncomfortable as he stood outside.

"Oh, I'm so sorry. Yes, come in! We were expecting Oren, but it seems like you are the one to help us out."

Yona opened the door and stepped aside, allowing Galen to enter. As he walked through the kitchen and stepped into the living room, he was amazed to see 15 to 20 men, women, and children sitting around the room in silence as they waited to see who had come to the back door.

Yona made her entrance right behind him, reassuring the group that he was quite safe.

"Hi everyone. This is Galen, one of the 'escaped dissenters' you all heard so much about. He is here to lead you to safety. It appears that Oren has had some other matters to take care of."

Immediately, the group was on their feet wanting to shake hands with the man who had become a local hero. After all the introductions, Yona called Galen over to officially meet Ms. Bina.

"Galen, this is Ms. Bina, sister of Miss Haddie whom you know very well, from what I understand."

Galen instantly at ease as he reached out to shake hands. Instead of just shaking his hand, Ms. Bina stood, giving him an unexpected hug as she spoke.

"Galen! It is so wonderful to meet you! You know you are quite a legend around these parts!"

"Well, it is wonderful to meet you as well," he replied. "Any sister of Miss Haddie's is definitely like family to me! Miss Haddie spent quite a bit of time preparing me for this."

"So Galen, what are your plans for this newest group of dissenters?" Ms. Bina asked.

"Honestly, I don't really know much, but I'm confident that the light will direct us to the house of refuge Elemet has prepared. I only know I'm here to assist Oren with all the refugees now on the move," Galen explained. Then turning toward the group, Galen addressed them directly.

"I am so honored to meet all of you and will do my best to safely move you to the house of refuge where you will be protected. My only request is that you follow my directions exactly. I understand that there are a number of new enforcers roaming the trails throughout the forest. The good news is that we will not be making this journey alone, but

Elemet has sent his light to direct us and warn us if any danger is nearby.

"It shouldn't take us more than a day or two to arrive at this safe homestead, but during our travels I ask that you keep the conversations to a minimum so as to avoid drawing undo attention to ourselves. If there is danger at any point, I will signal you. Please follow my directions exactly, so we can all arrive safely. Do you all agree?"

The entire group nodded in concurrence with Galen's instructions. Turning back towards Yona and Ms. Bina, he asked, "Will you two be fine if I take this group now? Do you need anything before we go?"

"We will be just fine," Ms. Bina replied. "We have been protected thus far and I'm sure we will continue to be protected."

"There is one thing you might do for me," Yona added.

"And what is that?"

"If, in your travels, you happen to meet our village elder, Cobar, and his terrible son, Zelig, could you please inform them that I will never become Zelig's wife, no matter what?"

Galen was a little puzzled as to why Yona was telling him this.

"It's a long story," she explained, "but I have decided that when I want to get married, it will be to the man of my own choosing and not to anyone the village elders decide to put me with. I just wanted to say that out loud."

Immediately, Galen was reminded of Shoshanna's own struggles with the same issue. He and his friends had experienced a time of freedom while residing in the Eagles'

Nest, but he remembered that she and all the others he would be traveling with had not yet tasted of the freedom he now knew. Compassion rose up in him as he spoke to encourage Yona.

"Yona, let me tell you. This fight for freedom is one that I and my companions are absolutely committed to. There are many others, all over this island who are setting captives free. When this is all finished, I assure you that Elemet will have his way and the island of Kumani will not remain the same. And, if I do run into this Cobar and Zelig you speak of, I will certainly tell them that you, alone, will make your choice in marriage. The young men will decide for themselves what jobs they will take, and people everywhere will have the choice to live in the love and peace found in Elemet alone. That is what we are fighting for."

"Thank you, Galen. Your courage inspires me."

With that being said, Galen turned towards the group now gathering close to the back door and exited first before signaling the group to follow him as he followed the light.

Chapter Twenty-Eight

LOST AND FOUND

The moment Roany took his turn to step through the archway, he found himself in a very familiar region, his home village of Kieran, standing directly in front of the place he once called home. Only charred embers of the cabin remained.

"What happened here?" he wondered as he mindlessly kicked around the few remaining articles; yet unburned. Though it seemed like ages since he last had entered his home, the sight of its utter destruction caused a sick feeling to come over him. Chen had assured him his mother was fine; however, there still was a sense of grief and loss he couldn't shake.

Roany would have preferred being sent anywhere else, but there was no other indicator telling him where to go from here, so he continued walking through the rubble to see if there was yet anything of value he could salvage. As he moved slowly towards the region where his bedroom once stood, his foot hit something hard. Looking down, he noticed a blackened, small metal box covered with debris.

Bending over, he brushed off the top, revealing an unusual engraving. Memories flooded back from many years ago when he and Galen used to freely roam the forests around their village.

Pictures appeared in front of him as he relived the moment he and Galen first discovered the interesting box. Once they'd figured out how to open it, they found an old, rusted key inside. After cleaning it up, the two of them decided it must open something of great value, so they kept it. Roany volunteered to bring it to his home for safe keeping. To avoid his mother questioning him about it, he decided to hide it under one of the loose planks in the floor until he and Galen decided what to do with it. As boys often do, the box was soon forgotten as they eventually moved on to their next adventure.

While he studied the container, another clear memory returned to him—the exact location where they had first found the box. Intrigued by his discovery and with no other direction at the moment, Roany decided that he would simply return to that spot to see if anything else would be revealed.

Though still unclear as to the purpose of this discovery, he left the remains of his home and made haste to arrive at the location of his boyhood discovery. He wondered if this was another of Elemet's ways to direct his steps and reveal his assignment. As he made progress, he passed another site that was also completely burned down. It was the former home of Eber and Giza, Galen's parents.

Rather than feeling disheartened as he had at his home, he now felt a passion to help bring these injustices and destruction to an end. Calling out to Elemet while moving forward, Roany asked for greater clarity and the real purpose behind his return journey to a childhood play site.

Relieved to see the light directing his steps as he left Pacey and sweet Lahela's homestead in Elkin, Mendi was uncertain where the light was directing him. He only knew he had to move quickly with the information he had learned about Hamah's plans.

As he headed into the forest, he suddenly became aware of movement in the brush around him, so he quickly stepped aside, behind a tree. Puzzled why the light was not warning him as it had many times before, he waited to see who or what was creating the rustling. With his eyes upon the trail, Mendi watched, but saw nothing—until he turned around. He was face to face with a large man staring him down. He nearly jumped out of his skin in surprise!

"Uh, hi. I'm Mendi," he responded nervously. "I wasn't exactly expecting to see anyone on my journey."

"Hmm," the stranger responded as he looked him over. "You look very familiar for some reason." There were a few uncomfortable moments of silence as the stranger tried recalling where he had seen this man before. Immediately, it came back to him as he squinted his eyes suspiciously.

"Weren't you the snake sent to spy on my friends, Eber and Giza?"

"Yes, that would have been me, I'm sorry to say," Mendi answered, as he bowed his head. "I am not proud of what I used to do. I have learned a lot and hopefully changed a lot as well, especially since I have spent time with Miss Haddie."

"You're friends with Miss Haddie?"

"Yes. She set me straight on a lot of things and taught me the ways of the eagle," he explained. "I decided to yield my life to Elemet and now I am following the light as he directs."

"Okay. That explains why I was sent here to meet you. My name is Oren. People in these parts have referred to me as the Woodsman, as I am often ushering people to safety through these woods."

"Oren! Oh, Ms. Bina and Yona have told me about you and how you escorted Tanzi to their tea party! So glad to finally meet you, myself," Mendi said, while extending his hand in friendship.

"So, you are friends with them as well?" Oren asked.

"Oh yes! And, I have been helping them out by reporting what Cobar and Zelig have been planning. Which reminds me, I have some crucial information I learned while in the village of Elkin. I overheard that Hamah is on the move, heading towards the secret meeting of village elders organized by Cobar. He plans to surprise them all by showing up. I don't know what Hamah is preparing to do, but I feel this could be quite a dangerous situation. I wasn't sure who to tell or what could be done, but I knew I needed to leave Pacey's homestead immediately. This was probably so I could meet and inform you of what is going on."

"Well, well," Oren responded, smiling. "This is all becoming quite interesting. I think we may have an important part to play in this 'secret gathering.' Come on, Mendi. Let's follow the light and see what Elemet has planned for this event."

Mendi agreed, so the two men walked together towards the gathering of the village elders planned for that night. Oren had previously attended several of the meetings while undercover in the past, so he was very familiar with its "hidden" location. The light, now leading them, would help them avoid any enforcers protecting and guarding Hamah as he moved towards the same destination.

Though the idea of attending a meeting with the village elders and Hamah in the same room did not sound very appealing to Mendi, Oren's confidence influenced him greatly. He could tell this man had many more experiences than he had had at this point. Oren's extensive history in accomplishing exploits on behalf of Elemet left Mendi feeling in awe of such a man.

As they journeyed through the woods, the two men shared their history with each other, becoming better acquainted and increasingly more at ease. This was especially important as they needed that assurance before placing themselves in grave danger with Elemet alone directing their destinies.

When Shoshanna finally arrived at Eber and Giza's expanding homestead, she was quite surprised to see Galen arriving as well with his group of refugees gathered from Ms. Bina's home in the village of Chana. Behind her trailed a weary crowd of travelers from the hidden caves near Kieran. Both companies were greatly relieved to finally arrive at their destination.

"Galen! You're here!" Shoshanna exclaimed excitedly.

"Yes. That was quite an interesting adventure," he responded, as they both escorted their groups into the now massive refugee camp.

As they entered the grounds, they were surprised to see Tanzi, now happily serving their many guests, along with Eber and Giza. Things had become quite busy at the homestead as the families were each led to their own tent with bedding and basic needs taken care of. Those who had arrived earlier were assisting the newcomers in getting settled as well.

As Tanzi was finishing one of her many tasks, she happened to notice Galen standing amidst the new arrivals and rushed over to greet him.

"Galen! It is so wonderful to see you!" she said as she hugged him briefly. "If things weren't so hectic right now, I would love to sit down and tell you about the many changes in my life. I do want to say how sorry I am about all the trouble I caused you and your family so many months ago. I

203

was a very different person back then and experienced some very traumatic things myself before I came to meet Chen."

"You have met Chen as well?" Shoshanna asked in amazement. She had heard about Roany's mother on their long trip to the Eagles' Nest.

"Oh!" Galen suddenly realizing that Tanzi had never met Shoshanna before. "Tanzi, this is my very dear friend and companion, Shoshanna. We first met at Miss Haddie's homestead quite a while back."

"Wonderful to meet you, Shoshanna!" Tanzi replied, grabbing the young woman and giving her a hug. "Your father, Oren, has told me quite a lot about you. He was my escort when I moved from my home to here. He is a wonderful man!"

As she stepped back from the young woman, Tanzi suddenly noticed both the ring and its brilliant stone gracing her hand. "Oh, and what is this?" she asked, while lifting Shoshanna's hand closer for a better look. "A gift from someone special?"

Blushing, Shoshanna looked towards Galen with a smile before responding. "Yes, I would say it was a gift from someone very special."

Noticing the little interchange between Galen and Shoshanna, Tanzi quickly figured out what was going on and nodded approvingly. "So, back to our discussion of your father. I'm sure he would be thrilled to see you."

"And, I would be thrilled to see him again as well. I haven't seen him since our escape into the woods so very long ago. Is he here?"

"Actually, he is not. We were expecting him to be escorting one of the groups brought in, but he has not yet shown up," Tanzi answered.

This reminded Galen of someone he had not seen. "Have either of you seen Roany?" Galen asked. "He left shortly after me and I expected to see him by now."

When both Shoshanna and Tanzi indicated they had not yet seen him, Galen became concerned.

"There may be something going on that I need to assist with. I think I'm going to go look for them both."

"Not without me!" Shoshanna responded. "I can help as well."

"Galen, aren't you going to first come see your parents before you leave again?" Tanzi inquired.

"I don't think I have time," Galen explained. "I am sensing an urgency about this and need to move quickly," he replied. "Can you let them know that I will be back and can visit with them on my return trip? And yes, Shoshanna. Please come. We can talk as we go."

With that, the two friends headed back out into the woods to see where the light might lead them and to discuss the information given to her by Chen. Galen was immediately concerned for Azriel as well. Together, they took some time to petition Elemet on behalf of their friend before focusing on their own task.

Chapter Twenty-Nine

TIME TO MOVE

Slowly, his eyes opened while he took a couple of deep breaths. Everything ached. Still dazed and uncertain of where he was, Azriel tried to look around, but realized that mud and debris covered him. Working his hands free, he pushed aside the branches that had fallen over him as he struggled to remember where he was and what had happened.

With great effort, he managed to sit up so he could better examine the destruction. As he glanced around, he recalled the intense dive his eagle, Zuko, had taken to help dislodge the last beam holding back the waters at Camp Coshek. During the last moments of their descent, he lost his seating and fell into the reservoir.

"*Did we succeed?*" he wondered to himself. Grabbing a nearby branch, Azriel worked to remove the mud still holding him in place. As he dislodged his lower body from the mucky mess, he was relieved to find that no bones were broken and he only had a few cuts and bruises to deal with.

Once he was freed, he used the branch to act as a cane to help steady himself. He wondered how long he had been lying there while surveying the muddy mess he now stood in. With only foundational stones remaining from the buildings, he was able to figure out where the fire pit had once been. Gratefully, he saw that the fires causing the haze over the lowlands of Kumani had been completely extinguished. The released waters of the reservoir had demolished both the fires and the camp itself.

Glancing upward, Azriel dimly hoped he might catch sight of the eagles and his warriors, possibly circling above looking for him, but the skies were clear. When they were unable to see him, they must have surmised he was gone and returned back to the Eagles' Nest.

Without his eagle to help transport him, Azriel realized he would have to walk down towards the lowland on his own. This would not be an easy or quick journey.

With some rather deep cuts to take care of and the need for more provisions, Azriel decided to first take a look among the remains of the camp to see if there was anything of use that he could salvage. As he hobbled along, examining the debris, he suddenly wondered what had become of the enforcers when the deluge of water hit them.

Glancing around again, he looked for any signs of life. Just then he heard a deep moan coming from a pile of wreckage, wrapped around a nearby tree. As he moved closer to the source of the sounds, he spotted another body, buried under the rubble. Quickly, he worked to remove branches pinning the man down. Though this enforcer had once been shooting arrows at him and his men, this was a life that yet had value to Elemet, and Azriel was determined to help him, if he could.

"What am I doing?" Roany asked himself as he moved closer to the location where he and Galen had first discovered the key. Many years ago they had played there as children climbing in and around a large overgrown tree with its sprawling branches.

"I should be finding refugees and escorting them to safety and here I am looking at a tree!" he scolded himself. If it weren't for the light, clearly indicating the path before him, he would have turned in a completely different direction in hopes of meeting up with Galen and the others. As much as he was tempted to try his own way, all his experiences in his recent past reminded him that the light was to be trusted and would certainly lead him where he was most needed.

It wasn't too much longer before Roany spotted the hill where the ancient tree stood gallantly with its branches outstretched, overshadowing the entire summit. He knew he was to climb this hill. That was all.

As he ascended the steep knoll, he was reminded of the times when Galen and he scampered up the embankment to climb the tree and gaze down upon the villages below. Their startling discovery of the mystery key stirred up memories of a number of playful adventures where the key served as the component solving all their problems.

Roany had to laugh as he envisioned their imagined wild escapades, where the tree became their ship, taking them to exotic locations beyond the realm of Kumani. Their quests would lead them to other islands with hidden treasures only their secret key could open for them.

Once he reached its peak, Roany took a moment to catch his breath as he walked around the magnificent tree, admiring its enduring strength and beauty. Turning out from the tree trunk, Roany scanned the land below, surveying its greenery and beauty, something he didn't remember doing as a boy.

Suddenly, it dawned on him. The usual haze he had grown up with was clearly diminishing, allowing the land's natural splendor to be seen. Its view nearly took his breath away. Walking around to take a look from another angle, Roany's attention was drawn to a building that he had often overlooked, especially since it represented the hold fear had on so many of Kumani's residents. In the valley below, stood the prison where many dissidents had been confined prior to their "retraining" at Camp Coshek.

As he stared at the facility, he could feel a vibration coming from his pocket. Curious, he stuck his hand into his clothing and felt the key. Pulling it out, he discovered that the key was no longer rusty, coated with years of neglect. Instead the key glowed, pulsating with light as he held it in his hand.

"What is this?" he asked in shock. A deep voice responded to his question.

"Go set the captives free. It is time!"

The power and authority emanating from the light and voice surrounding him knocked Roany to his knees.

"Who are you?" Roany asked almost afraid to hear the answer.

"I am Elemet. I have called you to set the captives free. Go now, for all things are ready."

Roany was shaking, just like the key in his hand. He now knew his destination, but still wasn't certain how he was going to accomplish this seemingly impossible task. While still on his knees, Roany felt something new flood into him—an uncommon courage filled this man who once only dreamed about exploits.

No longer was he concerned about saving his own life. Visions of others still held by fear and control appeared. As he saw faces before him, an overwhelming sense of compassion filled him. Roany knew he could not leave the prisoners behind.

Soon the shaking subsided and the young man stood to his feet, knowing that he had everything needed to fully accomplish what he was being sent to do.

It was time.

Cautiously, the men traveled along the trails as directed by the light. Whenever movement of any sort was heard,

Oren showed Mendi how to step through the doorway leading into the realm of protection he often used. Quite a number of enforcers were moving in the same direction, so they had to be extra watchful as they headed towards the gathering place of the village elders deep in the woods.

Obviously, Hamah had sent out word for all his enforcers to join him as he crashed the secret meeting, organized by Cobar and the village elders. All Oren knew was that he and Mendi were to be there as well. Unsure of exactly what Elemet had in mind, the two men slowly made progress. Once they arrived, they would need to wait until it was completely dark. That is when the village elders would begin to arrive.

When Oren was confident that they were alone on the trail, he began asking Mendi some pressing questions.

"So tell me, how does one move from being a snake to one now serving Elemet?"

"Well, I was trained from the time I was young to be an informant," Mendi explained. "At the orphanage, they took note of my popularity among the other children and used that for their advantage. I guess I just stopped caring about how my favor with the enemy affected others."

"That's sad," Oren replied. "So what brought you to your senses?"

"I hate to say it, but it was a girl."

"Of course it was," the woodsman responded. "Any girl in particular?"

"Actually, it was Yona. Once I heard the desperation of her situation, I knew I had to try and help her," Mendi said.

"Meeting her kind of woke me up from my stupor so I could see the wickedness of this whole system for the first time."

"So Yona, Jessah's friend, is the one who was able to reach you?"

"And then Ms. Bina stepped in, followed by Miss Haddie. All I can say is 'wow,' was I deceived! It's time I did my part to help bring an end to all this control."

"Well, I can assure you, you will have a big part as we confront this Hamah," Oren responded. "So have you met him before?"

"I haven't actually met him face to face, but I overheard his plans as he threatened Cobar and the village elders. He is not someone I would want to challenge on my own, that is for sure," Mendi said. "He sounds like pure evil!"

"All I know is that it is time for this power struggle to end so that the people of Kumani can really be free," Oren added. "I'm willing to do whatever it takes to bring that tyrant to his knees. Enough is enough!"

"Yes, I agree," Mendi concurred. "The way of the eagle is the only path that leads to real freedom."

As they drew closer to the gathering place, Oren motioned for Mendi to be quiet and draw back into the bushes so he could look around the region for the best place for the two of them to hide until nightfall. Once he found the spot, he directed Mendi to join him.

"The last time I attended one of these meetings, Elemet provided a hooded garment for me to wear so I could blend in with the others," he explained. "You stay here while I see if we have robes provided once again."

While Mendi waited, he suddenly heard movement in the brush not far from him. He held his breath as the sounds seemed draw closer. After what seemed like ages, Oren returned, beaming with joy as he carried back four robes and two additional people with his arm wrapped around the shoulders of one.

"Mendi, this is my daughter, Shoshanna, and her friend, Galen. They have come to join us for this meeting!"

"Really?" Mendi was stunned. "Aren't you two some of the escaped dissenters I heard so much about?"

"I guess we are," Galen replied with a smile. "And I heard that you were once a snake and now you have become one of us."

"Yes, that's true. I am so honored to meet you," he said, while extending his hand towards Galen.

"Well, unfortunately I think that's all the time we have for introductions," Oren interrupted. "Some of the enforcers are beginning to arrive."

No sooner had he spoken, than men began gathering around the perimeter of the building, obviously awaiting further instructions. There was no greeting or small talk among the men, just a simple acknowledgement of one another as they stood, staring blankly into the forest. They were obviously under the influence of something that had complete control over them.

Sadly, the four watched as the enforcers slowly assembled on one side of the building. With sinking hearts, they observed increasing numbers of their enemies coming together.

Chapter Thirty

GETTING READY

Dusk was just beginning to settle in as Jessah walked the grounds surrounding Miss Haddie's cottage. The air around her was fresh and fragrant, so she took the time to admire the flowers, fruits, and vegetables growing profusely in this oasis of peace. However, this evening her attention was drawn to the vibrant purples, pinks, and golds filling the skies above. This was not the norm for the island of Kumani.

As she pondered the significance of the sky paintings, Miss Haddie came up alongside her.

"It's quite stunning, isn't it," Miss Haddie stated, while staring upward.

"Yes. It's so different from our normal sunsets," Jessah replied. "The skies are speaking something to us, aren't they?"

"They certainly are, child. They speak of something and someone much bigger than ourselves. The picture they are painting for us tonight tells of changes that are rapidly unfolding before us."

"I feel like something significant is happening tonight," Jessah observed. "Do you sense that as well?"

"Oh yes," Miss Haddie responded. "Purple speaks of deliverance and new authority being established. Tonight will be quite different for you as you visit Camp Shabelle. Is Malia ready for this?"

"I don't think she realizes how ready she is and honestly, I don't know if I am even ready. I keep thinking I'm just a girl. What difference could I possibly make?" Jessah asked, looking up into Miss Haddie's eyes of compassion.

"Jessah, you have to remember that you are absolutely not alone, not ever. You are going out on behalf of the one who painted these skies this evening. You have been given the task of simply representing him to all those children, and they are responding."

"Yes, they are responding," she agreed. "Are you sure you don't want to join me tonight?"

"Child, I have been given the task of training those now arriving at Eber and Giza's homestead. Elemet has given you this task because he knows you can walk it out. He has already told you what is about to happen, so you won't be afraid, right?"

"How did you know that?" Jessah asked. "I was told not to share it with anyone when Elemet told me about this evening many months ago."

"Elemet told me just enough so I wouldn't become concerned when you don't return tomorrow," Miss Haddie explained, as she put her arm around the young girl standing next to her. "You know, I have grown quite attached to you.

This is just as hard for me to release you as it is for you to go without my assistance."

Jessah snuggled into Miss Haddie's embrace, resting her head against her, drinking in the peace that flooded them. They both knew that when the sun arose tomorrow, many things would be quite different for them. The only thing they needed to do was, once again, fully trust Elemet in every matter.

On the other side of the island, Roany followed the light before him, weaving through the trees on little traveled paths, leading downward toward the village of Kieran. The sun was rapidly setting, so he hurried to arrive at his destination before nightfall, even though he still had no idea what he was to do once he got there.

He was still shaken from his recent encounter with Elemet. The sad faces of the people he saw in his vision remained with him as he moved closer to the edge of the forest behind the prison. Once he got as close as he dared, he hid behind a large tree where he could observe the back side of the prison without being seen.

From this vantage point, he could easily see the heavy vine Jessah had once climbed up to deliver Elemet's message to Galen. As he studied the height she climbed, his opinion of this young girl he had once met at Miss Haddie's cottage, grew immensely. "What a brave girl she was!" he thought to himself. "I'm not sure I would have been that confident at her age."

As he considered the stone wall before him, he noticed the key he carried was vibrating once more, so he took it out of his pocket to look at. He studied the key more closely and noticed the top was heart-shaped with intricate designs embedded on either side of the heart. Though he had no idea what those designs indicated, he decided to place the heart shape in front of one eye. There was a hole in the center of the heart which appeared to be clear. Curiously, he felt prompted to hold up to his eye and look through it.

It took a moment for his eye to adjust, but as he continued staring through it, something appeared to glisten on the stone wall next to the vine. The longer he stared, the clearer the object appeared, until he could make out an outline of a door on the wall. When he looked over the top of the key, he saw nothing. But when he looked through the heart, the outline of the door appeared clearly.

While studying the shape of the door, he wondered if there was also a keyhole. Though none was visible, he thought maybe one would appear if he inserted the key where a keyhole might be.

"*This is silly!*" he said to himself, while shaking his head at the child-like nonsense that was running through his mind. "*An invisible door with an invisible keyhole!*" However, as he recalled all the steps leading to his hiding place behind the prison, including his encounter with Elemet, he had to admit that all of this was beyond the logical reasoning of his own mind. *"Why not an invisible door and keyhole?"* he asked himself.

As he was still musing about his discovery of the invisible door, a prison guard happened to walk by, making his normal rounds and checking the security of the back wall. Roany held his breath, keeping as still as possible until the guard passed his location. He was grateful that it was growing darker by the moment, which would allow him greater ease to check out this hidden entrance to the prison.

Roany waited patiently behind the tree until he felt it was sufficiently dark for him to make his move. Grabbing the key tightly in his hand, he moved as silently as possible until he stood beside the vine where he had seen the outline of the door. Bringing the key closer to the stone wall, he noticed the outline of the door became very apparent, but still there was no indication of a keyhole that he could see.

Not wanting to linger too long on the outside of the prison, he decided to insert the key in the general vicinity of where he imagined a keyhole would be. To his amazement, he found the key easily slipped inside what must have been a keyhole. He slowly turned the key and watched as the door opened before him. Though still quite uncertain of what he would do once inside the prison, he pulled the key out, and taking a deep breath, stepped through the doorway to see what might happen.

Though cut and bruised himself, Azriel determined that the man he had rescued from the mud and debris was in greater need than himself at the moment. Silently, he cried out to Elemet for help in this desperate situation. Immediately, he was reminded of the fresh spring that was running above where the reservoir had once been. He doubted the man would be able to make even that short journey in his weakened state, so Azriel had him lay down on some brush, just above the muddy mess, assuring him he would return with fresh water.

As he pressed through the washed out areas, he caught sight of a bucket he could use to haul the water back. Moving uphill caused every muscle to ache as he forced himself to continue making progress, until he finally reached the clean water. Gratefully, he leaned over, splashing water first onto his face and then into his parched mouth.

Not wanting to keep the wounded man waiting too long, Azriel filled the bucket and returned to him as quickly as he could. Tearing off a piece of his own shirt, Azriel poured some of the water over the cloth, using it to wash the man's face. Gently, he lifted his new friend up, just enough so he could get a sip of water.

Once his thirst was quenched, Azriel decided to see if this enforcer was able to converse yet.

"Hey! How are you doing? Feeling any better?" Azriel could see the man wanted to communicate, but was still coming out of a drug-induced fog.

"My name is Azriel," he continued. "I've been checking you out and it seems like your arm might be injured, possibly broken, but maybe I can find something to use as a sling. Does that sound okay?"

The man nodded. This encouraged Azriel greatly. "Any chance you can tell me your name first? I just want to know what to call you."

With difficulty, the man slowly moved his mouth and whispered, "Jovan."

"Your name is Jovan?" Azriel repeated. The man nodded again. "Ok, Jovan. I'm going to see if I can find something we can use for a sling. I'll be right back."

After several minutes of searching, Azriel returned with what appeared to be a shirt, large enough to place around the man's arm and around his neck. Though wet and soiled, it would work. Once the sling was in place, Azriel helped Jovan sit up.

"Well, that is better. We can take things slowly as you are able to move."

"Thank you, Azriel," the man replied. "So, where am I?"

"You don't know where you are?"

Jovan shook his head.

"Do you remember anything about the battle we had here?"

"Nothing," Jovan answered.

"Do you realize you were working as an enforcer?" The man looked at Azriel in shock.

"Me? If anything, I was a dissenter and that's why I was sent to prison. I don't remember much after that. So where are we?"

"This is what remains of Camp Coshek and you were working here for a man named Hamah. We believe he was experimenting with a number of herbs which he used to drug his enforcers so they would do his bidding without question," Azriel explained.

"Wait! I have a wife and child! Do you know where they are?"

"I don't, but I'm sure we can find them, once we get out of here," Azriel assured him. "Why don't you wait here and rest a little more while I see if I can locate my eagle, Zuko. I don't think we are in any condition to walk all the way down into the lowlands."

"You have an eagle?" he asked in astonishment.

"Well, either I have an eagle or he has me," Azriel joked. "I will be right back."

As Azriel walked away, he could already feel new strength flowing into his sore body.

"Thank you, Elemet," he whispered, heading up towards a hilltop where he could better see the horizon.

Once on the high point, he scanned the skies, looking for any sign of Zuko. He knew that Zuko would most likely return, looking for his handler. As Azriel had been unconscious for a period of time, he had no idea how much time had passed since their attack on Camp Coshak.

Putting his fingers to his mouth, he let out a shrill whistle. No sign of the eagle at all. Azriel whistled, several more times, hoping to attract the eagle's attention. Still nothing. As he shielded his eyes from the setting sun, he scanned the land below, looking for any indication of what might be happening.

He did notice that the haze had already begun to diminish. That was good. Though still sore, Azriel was anxious to help out all his friends facing the challenges below, but there was nothing he could do at this moment. He decided the best he could do was to find some food and temporary shelter for both himself and Jovan. A little discouraged, Azriel walked back down the hill to care for his friend as they awaited help.

It would be a long night.

Chapter Thirty-One

ON YOUR MARK

I t was quite early as Uri finished up his final rounds in checking the security of Camp Shabelle. He snickered to himself as he considered the pointlessness of his endeavors, especially since the real threat to this crumbling system was already in position, simply waiting for the call to move. Though he had not been updated recently, he remembered Chen's promise that his steps would be clearly directed when the time came.

Already, he had a sense in his heart that the time to act was drawing close. As he moved around checking locked doors, he suddenly caught sight of a youngster, moving about the hallways.

"Jessah?" he thought to himself. He quickened his pace to catch up with her, but as he turned the corner, she was no longer in sight. Puzzled, he wondered where she had gone. As he looked around, he felt a slight tap on his back. Turning around, he looked down at the young girl, looking more and more mature every time he saw her.

"Girl, how did you do that?" Uri asked in surprise. "I just saw you walk by, and then you were gone!"

Jessah smiled, shyly. "Elemet has given me a new gift for today," she explained. "I can step into a place of protection any time I need to. I was just testing it out when you came looking for me. Do you like it?"

"Yes!" Uri answered. "Very effective indeed! So, is today the day we have been waiting for?"

"I believe it is. All I know is that I won't be returning to Miss Haddie's this morning as I usually do. I am to remain here for a time getting everything ready."

"What do I need to do to help you?" Uri asked.

"I think you will be directed to open the doors for us when the time comes and then make sure that Miss Moselle and her staff do not interfere," Jessah replied. "The light will direct you at the right time. For now, I must wake up the other children and make sure they will be ready. I'm excited to see what Elemet has planned."

"So am I! I guess I will see you later."

"Yes, you will. Today is the day!" With that, Jessah turned and continued down the hallway to visit the various dorms where the children were still sleeping. Uri returned to his rounds. Moving down the corridor, he suddenly noticed the light leading him in a different direction than normal. His heart beat excitedly as he was ready for some real action!

"Okay. Let's do this!" he whispered to himself.

On another part of the island, Roany moved silently down the hallways of the prison he had entered. The guards were sleeping heavily as he slipped past them to the first floor where some of the prisoners were slumbering as well. With new instructions recently given to him by Elemet, he knew exactly what he had been sent to do.

Walking up to the first door, he lifted the glowing key in his hand and unlocked it. As he pushed it open, he quietly roused the prisoners, letting them know that once all the other inmates were awakened, he would be leading them out. Smiles broke across their faces as they sat up, awaiting further instructions.

"I will be back soon," Roany instructed them as he moved on to the next door. Going from door to door, in a rather short time, Roany had unlocked all the doors in the entire prison. As the inmates began filing out behind him, he led them to the hidden back door he had entered through. Once they were all assembled, Roany gave them clear instructions as to where they needed to go first.

"If you break ranks and head off on your own prematurely, I cannot guarantee your safety. It is very important that all of you follow these instructions exactly. There are a great many things going on at this time. Many more enforcers are moving around and if we are not wise, we all could be caught and dealt with very harshly. There is a plan for us to enter into complete freedom—if we will stay together. Do you understand?"

The men nodded in agreement as Roany pushed open the door, leading them out into the darkness. As soon as they had exited the prison, a light appeared before Roany, directing them. Behind the men, only empty cells and sleeping guards remained.

It was quite late before the village elders began arriving, under cover of darkness, while donning the usual hooded garbs to hide their identities. As soon as Oren and the others saw the elders entering the building, all four dissenters put on their own garbs to join the assembly.

As they slipped inside with the elders, they could sense the growing tension which filled the room. None of others were aware of the gathering enforcers hidden close by in the trees outside. Once all had arrived, the dissenters were certain that Hamah would make his grand entrance after the meeting was well underway. Clear instructions were brewing with the four disguised dissenters. Elemet had plans of his own.

Soon the full assembly had arrived, but with the added anxiety surrounding this secret gathering, no one had noticed the additional "elders" who had infiltrated their meeting. Once all were seated, Cobar stood and walked to the front. He cleared his throat before beginning.

"Gentlemen, you have been called together for us to discuss a rather disturbing turn of events, one which I hope we can resolve as quickly as possible. I'm sure you have all heard of the burning of Yashen and unfortunately, there were no survivors, just as Sir Hamah predicted at our last gathering."

"Sadly, that is not the end of our problems," Cobar continued, while attempting to sound as calm and confident as possible. "Right after the burning of Yashen, I was visited by Sir Hamah himself. He has informed me that some radical changes are about to take place, which may or may not be a bluff. Of course, I am hoping that it is a bluff, but you need to be informed of what he has said."

"Would you just get on with it!" one of the elders demanded. "What did he say?"

"Well, he has told me that even as we speak, new poisons are already filling our atmosphere and deadly toxins are flooding all of our water sources."

Immediately, all the elders began shouting their objections and fears out loud. Cobar had to overpower them forcefully by barking out orders for silence so he could continue. Eventually the talking subsided enough, allowing him to finish.

"Now, if this is true, Sir Hamah informed me that only he has the herbal antidote needed for us to continue our positions as village elders. This antidote will be distributed by him alone, providing we submit to his plans for the future of Kumani."

"And what are his plans for Kumani?" another elder asked.

"Well, apparently he wants to eliminate some of the smaller villages and bring everyone closer together so it will be easier for him to monitor—and he wants us to refer to him now as 'Lord Hamah.'"

The room exploded in angry shouts as the elders scoffed at 'Lord Hamah's' audacity.

"Who does he think he is?" one elder clamored angrily.

"He has no right to threaten us like that!" another hollered out.

"What are we going to do about this treacherous man?" someone else asked.

"He has to be stopped!" a man called out.

"That is exactly why I have invited you here," Cobar stated emphatically. "We need to figure out what can be done to stop this man, Hamah. Unfortunately, we must also determine a way to deal with him and his own personal enforcers. They do his bidding without any consideration of what is right and what is wrong."

"Exactly!" responded a calm voice from one entering the door of the building. It was Lord Hamah himself with a sick smirk upon his face. The room grew silent in fear as Lord Hamah sauntered up to the front while he continued speaking.

"I have already considered all the options you might come up with. Let me assure you, there is no way to stop what has already been done. Your only hope for survival now is submitting to me alone."

"And what if we don't?" an elder shouted out defiantly.

"Well, you will soon find yourself feeling less and less clear, until your brain is little more than mush. At that point, I will decide who is to remain alive and who is unnecessary for the survival of Kumani. The good news is that you will no longer care when I decide your fate."

Finally, Oren could hold his peace no longer and stood.

"Not all of us are afraid of your vain threats!" he announced.

"You call my threats 'vain'?" Hamah asked incredulously. "Was my burning of Yashen vain?"

Quickly, Galen also stood to his feet and responded boldly.

"Yes, you won one battle, but the war is not over. We're here to announce your defeat."

"My defeat?" Hamah almost laughed. "Do you know what is awaiting all of you the moment you try to leave this building?"

Shoshanna also joined Galen and her father in standing, but drew back her hood, revealing her face as she spoke.

"There is nothing awaiting any of us outside the doors of this building," she announced, "for they have all been taken care of." Mendi stood as well, with the other three as all of them drew back their hoods.

"Dissenters!" Hamah responded in shock. "We'll take care of this now. Enforcers!"

"They are not coming," Shoshanna replied confidently as her invisible warriors had already been sent to take care of the men waiting outside. "They have been detained."

At this point, Mendi spoke up. "And, we are not actually dissenters, but citizens of another reality, the way of the eagle, led by Elemet himself."

Hamah, absolutely flustered by their defiance, ran to the door to call for his enforcers once again, but instead, was met by a man he had never seen before. Though dirty with bruises and cuts still showing, this man's bold confidence caused Hamah to back up. Azriel stepped in front of him and entered the building.

He had something to say.

"I have just come from Camp Coshek where Hamah did indeed plan on poisoning both the atmosphere and our waters with his concoctions. However, by the grace of Elemet, my men and I were successful in destroying both the smoking fires and the toxic reservoir intended to poison our waters. All that Hamah has planned has been eradicated."

"It can't be!" Hamah objected.

"Oh, it can be and is," Azriel replied. "And here is one of your former enforcers to confirm what I have said." Jovan stepped into the room, still wearing the blue shirt identifying him as one of Hamah's enforcers, with a dirty sling holding his broken arm. He spoke out clearly for all to hear.

"My name is Jovan. I was once arrested as a dissenter from the village of Elkin and then I was taken to Camp Coshek. Though I don't remember much of what was done to me, I will testify that Camp Coshek is now totally demolished. The reservoir with poisoned waters was diverted and has completely extinguished the fires which previously created the haze we had all become accustomed to. This man, Azriel, saved my life and has brought me here on the back of his eagle so we could inform you all of this marvelous victory."

"No, no, no!" Hamah screamed. "It can't be true!" As he continued his tirade, Oren, Galen, and Mendi stepped up to help escort Hamah to a place of confinement until it could be decided what to do with him.

Meanwhile, the elders quickly made their exit from the building, scattering in every direction. As they left, they couldn't help but glance at the enforcers held back by an invisible barrier of the warriors accompanying Shoshanna.

Cobar was one of the escaping elders, trying not to draw too much attention to himself. As the sun was just beginning to peak over the horizon, an exhausted Cobar hurried into his home, calling Zelig as he entered.

Sleepily, Zelig came out of his room with disheveled hair, confused by all the commotion.

"Quick, grab your things. We need to move right now. Things have gotten out of control!"

"What? What are you talking about? Didn't you and the elders figure out how to take care of Hamah?" Zelig objected.

"He has been taken care of, but not by us. I'll explain later. Hurry now and grab some things so we can get out of here before we are tracked down!"

"Tracked down by who? And what about Yona? I still want her!"

"We can grab Yona on our way out, but we need to move quickly if we want to avoid them," Cobar replied.

"Avoid who?" Zelig demanded again.

"The dissenters! They said something about Elemet and the way of the eagle. I don't know. Mendi was even there!"

"Mendi? That weasel informant? What threat could he be?"

"I don't understand it, but he has changed. Something is going on here and we need to leave!"

Okay, okay. I'm packing. You can explain all this to me later."

Chapter Thirty-Two

MAKING THEIR MOVE

S hortly after the village elders emptied the building, eleven other eagles with their riders descended into the clearing in front of the building used by the elders for their secret gatherings. Immediately, the warriors dismounted, joining Oren, Galen, and Mendi as they prevented Hamah from escaping. As the other warriors entered the building, Keoni stopped in front of Azriel, giving him a welcome back hug.

"I'm so glad to see you!" Keoni declared. "We all saw you fall into the water and when you didn't resurface, we thought we had lost you!"

"I thought I was done as well," Azriel admitted. "I don't remember much after hitting the water, but when I finally came to, I knew there had to be a purpose for me to survive such a fall, and there was. Keoni, let me introduce you to Jovan. Miraculously, he also survived the waters."

"Glad to meet you, Jovan," Keoni said while extending his hand in greeting. Noticing his left arm in a sling and both men still filthy with obvious cuts and bruises, he continued. "It looks like you and Azriel could use a little care right now. We will see that you both are taken care of as soon as this 'Lord Hamah' is taken to a secure facility."

"Thank you," Jovan responded. "Even with the injuries, I am beginning to feel more and more like myself. I appreciate your kindness." Keoni nodded in response just as the warriors were coming out with Hamah safely in handcuffs.

The first rays of the sun were just beginning to break through the darkness when a loud trumpet blast was heard across the land. Everyone froze and listened as the sound waves washed across the island of Kumani, driving all the remaining haze out to sea.

The corralled enforcers were the first to respond to the clarion call of freedom. Slowly, the invisible warriors began releasing their hold on them as they dropped to their knees. The effects of the drugs upon their minds began receding as the former enforcers started recalling who they were and where they came from.

It was in the midst of this birthing of new freedom that Shoshanna, Oren, Galen, and Mendi finally emerged from the building. They, too, had heard the trumpet blast and were amazed as they began seeing its effect upon the former enforcers. However, they did not have much time to enjoy the beginnings of their victory as all four were suddenly impressed with yet another unfolding battle that needed their attention.

Unsure of where they were going, they cried out to Elemet for wisdom, and direction on their next assignment. They had not yet seen Roany and sensed that he would shortly be needing their assistance.

As they discussed their options, Oren suddenly saw what he had been looking for—a doorway appearing near the trees.

"Follow me," Oren instructed them. "I believe we have our means of transportation. In the past, these doorways were only used as a safe place for me to hide when a threat was nearby, but now I think we are going to be sent where we are needed."

"Father, that is amazing!" Shoshanna replied excitedly. "That is exactly how we arrived here from the Eagles' Nest. Let's do this!"

"Wait!" Galen interjected. "I feel as though we might all be sent to different locations as we have been in the past. I just want to remind you of that."

"Really?" Mendi responded. He was still very new at this, so he had many questions, but there was no time to answer them.

"We just need to trust Elemet and where he sends us," Shoshanna explained. "When we get to our destinations, we will better understand what it is we are to be doing."

"Is that the way it always is? Trust first, and then find out what Elemet wants to do?" Mendi asked.

"Don't worry," Galen responded with a smile. "You'll get used to it. We do need to get moving. So Oren, where is that doorway?"

"Follow me," he said. "I'll go through first, and then each of you can follow."

The three young adults walked over to a large tree as Oren indicated where they needed to go. Once he stepped through, he completely vanished from sight. Next, Mendi was encouraged to go, followed by Shoshanna. Finally it was Galen's turn as he stepped through to wherever he was needed.

Meanwhile, across the island in Camp Shabelle, things were getting stirred up as well. They had also heard the trumpet blast. Sleeping children throughout the dorms were being aroused by Jessah and Malia. Though it was still early, the children had been prepared and got up quickly. One young boy, only 5 years old, came up to the two girls, still clinging to his thin, worn-out blanket.

"Is this really the day you have been telling us about?"

"Oh yes, Eliam," Malia assured him. "This is the day we have been talking about. You need to hurry and get dressed so you can be ready."

"But once we are ready, where will we go?" Eliam asked, quite puzzled. Jessah, seeing his concern, bent over and looked the boy in his sparkling eyes.

"We will all go out and be free," she said with a smile. "Now hurry. Okay?"

"Okay!" he responded with a large grin as he returned to his bunk to get dressed.

Uri could hear the stirring of the children as he walked down the corridor, unlocking every door he came to. In the midst of his task, he suddenly heard a familiar voice, one he had hoped would not be aroused as well.

"Uriah!"

"Yes, Miss Moselle."

"Did you hear that terrible noise outside? It sounded like something coming from the mountains."

"Yes, ma'am," he replied. "I heard it. Not sure what it was, though."

"Well, it's good to see you are double checking all the doors," she said. "We don't want any strangers breaking into our facility."

"No, ma'am," he responded. "I'm in the midst of rechecking all the doors right not. Everything should be just fine." Even as he assured her, he was already receiving insight on how he could delay Miss Moselle and her staff so the children could make their move.

"Oh, by the way, the cook told me she wanted to treat you and your staff to a special breakfast before all the children came in for theirs," Uri stated. "I have been smelling it all morning. Must be something really great. Do you want me to notify the staff for you?"

"My, my. Isn't that nice," she answered. "Yes, please let all the staff know so we can meet in the kitchen for breakfast. Thank you. I'll hurry and get ready then."

Under his breath, Uri spoke as Miss Moselle walked off. "Yes, you hurry and get ready. You will have a big surprise very shortly."

As soon as Miss Moselle left, Uri made an appeal to Elemet for some extra help in setting up the surprise. He then rushed down the hall, just in time to catch all the staff as they were entering the front door, preparing for their work day.

When they entered, Uri greeted them and then directed them towards the kitchen where their very special breakfast awaited. Already, luscious aromas of freshly baked sweet rolls, steaming bacon, fried potatoes, and scrambled eggs were making their way down the hallway. The smells created such a desire in them they could hardly wait to arrive in the kitchen. Innocently, Uri followed behind the staff and was pleased to see Miss Moselle eagerly showing up for the "breakfast bash" now awaiting them.

When the door was pushed open, Uri's eyes grew wide as he looked upon the spread set before them in the kitchen. Yes, Elemet knew how to throw a party, especially when a distraction was needed. Once all the "guests" were safely inside, Uri quietly stepped back out of the kitchen, locking the door behind him. Again, he looked upward requesting that any keys the staff had would not work.

Smiling and whistling as he went, Uri headed back down the corridor towards the dorms to see if the children had need of assistance.

"Hurry up, Zelig!" Cobar barked roughly. "We have to get there before most of the residents wake up."

Behind him, Zelig struggled with the cart he was pulling. Piled up with all the "essential things" they would need to set up a new home somewhere deep in the forests, away from anyone who might recognize them.

"You know, this might go a little faster if you would help me pull this thing," Zelig suggested.

"Yes, it might," Cobar agreed, "but then if anyone saw a chief village elder working like that, they might think I have surrendered my position of leadership. Also, remember we are going to get your bride right now and one of us needs to be fresh when we pick her up."

"But, father, most people don't even know you are a village elder!"

"It doesn't matter. I still have to keep up my image, at least, as a business owner," he responded impatiently. "Stay focused. We are getting closer to our first destination."

Once they found a safe place to camouflage their cart behind bushes, Cobar went over the instructions one more time so that Zelig was clear on what he needed to do. When everything was ready, Cobar went up to a back door and pounded loudly before moving quickly out of sight.

It took a little while for someone to respond and just as they anticipated, the young woman stepped outside to see if someone was nearby. The moment she did, Zelig snapped into action and grabbed the young woman while muffling her screams with a drug-soaked cloth placed over her face. As he held her, she eventually stopped struggling and her entire body went limp.

Cobar boldly walked up and shut the door so they could be on their way without further delay. As Zelig tied up her hands and feet and then gagged her, his father pulled the cart out so her body could be placed inside where she couldn't be seen. Once loaded, they quickly covered her up with a blanket before anyone could see what they had done.

But someone had seen them.

A small boy came walking out from among the trees and stood in front of the cart.

"What are you doing?" he asked innocently.

"Nothing, boy," Cobar replied gruffly. "Now step aside."

"I saw you put someone in your cart. Who was that?"

"You didn't see anything, boy! Now move or we will run you over with this cart!" Zelig threatened him. However, instead of moving, the child began pointing at the cart.

"I saw you tie her up and put her in the cart," he said, unmoved by their threats. "Why did you do that?"

Just as Zelig was preparing to push the boy aside, another girl also stepped out from the dense bushes surrounding the back of the cabin. The only path wide enough to accommodate their cart was now blocked by the children.

"Yes," she said, while strolling up next to the boy and putting her arm around him, "why did you do that?"

Both Cobar and Zelig were becoming infuriated with these children and their interference with their plans.

"Look! You don't know who I am, but I'm warning you both to step aside now or you could get hurt!" Cobar shouted.

"Oh, I know who you and what you are trying to do," the girl responded confidently. "And it's not going to work."

Angrily, Zelig dropped the front of the cart and moved towards the children. Picking up the boy, he set him off to the side, out of their way, but the girl simply folded her arms while continuing to stand her ground.

Suddenly, the back door of the cabin swung open as an elderly lady poked her head out.

"Yona! Yona! Where did you go?" she called. As she peered out, she suddenly realized there was a loaded cart sitting at her back door with two men and two children standing by it. It took a moment for her to recognize who they were.

"Cobar! Zelig! What are you doing at my back door? You two have no business being here!" she told them.

Zelig, turning towards his father said, "I thought you said she was blind!"

Cobar, clearly confused by what he was seeing, turned the question directly to Ms. Bina.

"I thought you were blind!"

"I was, but my sight suddenly returned and I am glad!" Squinting her eyes a bit to take a better look at the children, she recognized the girl.

"Jessah! My word! What are you doing with these two snakes?"

"I'm preventing them from leaving," she responded. "They have something that does not belong to them."

"What?" Ms. Bina replied. "What have they taken?"

Immediately, another figure stepped out from behind the trees and joined Jessah in front of the cart.

"Yes, Cobar," the woman added. "What have you taken now?"

"Shoshanna!" he exclaimed. "I will not let women and children stop me. Get out of our way or we will walk right over you!"

"Go ahead and try," Shoshanna calmly replied.

Determined not to be outdone by them, Cobar shouted for Zelig to pull the cart forward as he pushed from behind, but it would not budge. They tried several times, unsuccessfully, with both their faces growing redder from all their efforts.

"What have you done to our cart?" Cobar shouted angrily.

"The question we need to ask is what have you done?" Shoshanna replied.

Realizing that they would not be able to escape with the cart, both men attempted to run off on their own, but found they were also hindered by some unseen force.

"What is going on here?" Cobar asked, in complete frustration.

Looking towards the trees behind them, Shoshanna called out. "Mendi, why don't you come out and join us? Maybe you can look inside that cart to see what these men were attempting to take."

Mendi came walking out calmly, approached the cart, and threw off the blanket they had placed over it. He glanced at both men angrily before gently lifting a very groggy Yona from the cart.

"Yona!" Ms. Bina cried out in concern. "Mendi, carry her inside so we can attend to her." After Mendi carefully carried Yona past the old woman into her cabin, Ms. Bina turned back to the men, still stuck by the cart.

"Cobar and Zelig, I knew you were a couple of snakes from the beginning, but this is beyond audacious. It is downright criminal! May Elemet deal with you appropriately!" she said as she turned to reenter her cabin.

"Are you going to tell us by what magic you are holding us here?" Zelig asked Shoshanna.

Walking over to the little boy who was still watching with wide eyes, she bent down to peer into his face before responding.

"It is no magic, but simply authority granted to me by Chen, himself," she replied. Then addressing the boy, she asked, "And, what is your name?"

"My name is Eliam."

"Hi Eliam. My name is Shoshanna." The boy beamed back at her. "And where did you come from?"

Jessah, who was just beginning to feel more comfortable, moved from her stance in front of the cart to join Shoshanna.

"He came with me on this little adventure," she explained. "He wanted to join me after we left Camp Shabelle, so I brought him."

"Oh! You are a very special boy indeed!" Shoshanna told him.

"I have no parents," he added. "And I just wanted to see where Jessah was going."

"Well, I am so glad you came," Shoshanna answered. "You are a very brave boy!"

Eliam smiled and threw his arms around Shoshanna as she pulled Jessah into the hug as well.

Sarcastically, Cobar interrupted their conversation.

"When you are done with your little child's play, can you tell me who Chen is and when we will be able to move again."

"Chen is the one to whom you will have to give an account to," she explained. "He and his father, Elemet, are the real rulers of this island. As far as your freedom goes, I am awaiting the rest of our team who will be here shortly, I am sure. Until then, you get to enjoy the company of my assigned warriors who are holding both you and the cart in place."

"What warriors are you speaking of?" Zelig added. "There is no one here with you!"

"Really?" Shoshanna replied. "Eran, would you mind making you and your men visible to our prisoners?"

The moment Shoshanna spoke, twelve huge warriors became visible to the entire group. Eliam gasped as he studied the warriors in their gleaming armor, holding both the cart and the two men in place.

Cobar literally shook in fear as one fierce warrior appeared looking downward, directly towards his face, while massive hands refrained him from moving at all. The warrior was twice his size, wearing a heavy metal breastplate made of both gold and silver. Hanging from his side, a glistening sword, still in its sheath, made it abundantly clear that no flattering words or emotional appeals would stop him from performing his duties, whatever they might be.

Zelig, too, found himself speechless as two of the warriors stood in front of both him and the cart handles he was still holding. He wanted to release the handles, but he could not move. When he looked up briefly into their stony faces, the intensity of their stares was more than he could handle, so he cast his gaze downward. Terror rose up within him, but unable to move or hide from their presence, he breathed heavily to keep from being overcome by panic.

After being assured everything was taken care of, Shoshanna continued. "Why don't we three go inside to see how Yona is doing? These two men aren't going anywhere for a while."

Just as Eliam, Jessah, and Shoshanna were preparing to enter the cabin, Galen and Roany showed up with the escaped prisoners. Shoshanna and Jessah both approached Galen, Roany and their new friends with hugs of excitement.

"I knew you would be here," Shoshanna said, "And look what we have saved for you. Galen and Roany, you both remember Cobar, but you might not know his son, Zelig. These two have quite a history here. Jessah and little Eliam caught them as they attempted to take something that did not belong to them."

From his position at the back door of the cabin, the boy called out, "They tried to take Yona."

"Wow! Great job all of you!" Galen responded. Looking at the burly warriors still holding Cobar and Zelig, he had to laugh. "Your warriors have certainly come in handy, haven't they?"

"They sure have!" Shoshanna agreed. "And who are all these other men traveling with you?"

"These are wonderful men, once arrested as dissenters, but now they are here to help us," Roany explained. "I'm sure they will be more than eager to help escort both Cobar and Zelig to the proper prison until Chen decides what to do with them."

"Oh yes!" one man responded. "We will be happy to escort them wherever you need them to go."

"How wonderful!" Shoshanna exclaimed. "Why don't you all come in for some refreshment before you head out?"

"You don't have to ask us twice!" Roany answered. "Come on in, men!"

The entire group celebrated as they entered into the cabin. Once again, the room grew to accommodate the guests, while Cobar and Zelig remained frozen in position, awaiting their arrest.

Chapter Thirty-Three

THE SOUNDS OF FREEDOM

Things appeared quite blurry as the young woman blinked repeatedly, struggling to pull herself out of unconsciousness and into reality. Slowly, her clarity and focus returned only to realize that she was the object of intense scrutiny from a number of dear friends. A cup of Miss Haddie's tea was quickly offered as she attempted to sit up. Questions arose in her mind, but no words could be formed yet, so she just sat and sipped as she tried to process all that was being said around her.

"Yona, I'm so glad you are doing better!" Jessah said as she moved to sit next to her. "I was so angry when I saw what they had done to you! I was not going to let them escape until help arrived! That's when Shoshanna showed up. You should have seen her, Yona! She stood up to Cobar and Zelig with so much boldness! Wow!"

At the mention of Shoshanna's name, Yona finally was able to respond. "Wait! Did you say, Shoshanna? Is she here?"

"Yes, I'm here, Yona," Shoshanna answered, putting her face close enough so Yona could see her. "And I'm so glad you are here with us as well. We were quite concerned about you for a little while. How are you feeling?"

"My head feels like it's spinning a little, but it's getting better," Yona replied. "So, I'm confused. What happened to me? The last thing I remember was someone pounding loudly on our back door. I thought it might be villagers looking for shelter, so I answered the door."

"Apparently, that knocking came from those snakes, Cobar and Zelig," Ms. Bina explained. "They tried to kidnap you, had you drugged, and tied up in their cart. They would have taken off too, if Jessah and little Eliam hadn't arrived when they did."

"Who is Eliam?" Yona inquired. "Have I met him?"

"Not yet," Jessah replied, while grabbing the young boy's hand and pulling him close to Yona. "He's my new little friend from Camp Shabelle, which is now empty of all the children."

"It is! That is wonderful, but where are all the other children, and who is taking care of them?"

"Oh." Jessah stopped to think about who was with the children when she left. "I think Uri is still with them, along with Malia, my other friend who helped me train all the children before they were released. I felt such an urgency to get to your cabin, I just grabbed Eliam and left. Wait! I think I saw Oren appear just as I was getting ready to leave. Yes, Oren is definitely with them."

"Uri and my father are babysitting a bunch of free-spirited orphans? That has got to be a sight to see!" Shoshanna laughed. "I cannot imagine either of them knowing what to do with all those children!"

After having a good laugh at the thought of two inexperienced men handling newly-freed children, Galen suggested that it might be a good idea for everyone to step back outside so Yona could continue recovering. When everyone else filed out, Mendi stayed behind to speak with Yona.

"How are your wrists and ankles feeling?" he asked in concern. "They had you gagged and bound up tightly. When I carried you in, you were pretty limp. I untied you as quickly as I could."

"My wrists and ankles feel fine. Thank you, Mendi," Yona said, as she smiled weakly. "I'm so glad you were here to help me."

"Oh, it wasn't just me!"

"I know, but it means a lot to me that you were here when I needed you."

Sensing that Yona and Mendi needed a few moments alone, Ms. Bina decided she needed to check the hot water to make some more tea. As soon as she left, Yona continued.

"I've been thinking about all you said and all you have done to help me and Ms. Bina. I know I told you I wanted to be a child a little longer and not be forced into adulthood too soon, but after all we have been through, I was thinking maybe we could just continue being friends for a while? And, maybe after that…"

"You know, I was thinking the same thing," Mendi replied. "I've actually learned quite a bit since I last saw you. The fact is, I was thinking I might just stay around here in Chana to keep an eye on you two."

"That would be great!" Yona replied excitedly.

Just then Ms. Bina returned with two more cups of tea for both Yona and Mendi to enjoy. While serving the tea, she commented, "Now that you two have this whole friendship thing worked out, why don't you sit down for a little while, Mendi, and tell us all about your adventures since we last saw you."

"I would love that!" Mendi replied. "However, let me check with my friends to see if they need me anymore."

As Mendi stepped out the door, he saw the released prisoners escorting both Cobar and Zelig to the prison where they would be held for the time being. He joined Galen, Roany, Shoshanna, and Jessah as they continued to laugh about what they might see if they were to show up outside Camp Shabelle where the children would be playing. As they spoke, Eliam latched onto Shoshanna's hand and didn't appear as if he was willing to release it any time soon.

"So tell me, what is the plan?' Mendi asked.

"Well, now that Cobar and Zelig have been taken care of, Jessah informs us that Miss Moselle and her staff are still locked up in the kitchen, so we thought we might go there, see how Oren and Uri are holding up, and then escort Miss Moselle and the others to a prison until Chen deals with them," Galen responded.

"I gave the key to one dissenter with instructions that he opens all the village prisons in the surrounding villages," Roany explained. "And I'm pretty sure that Chen will have a general assembly for the residents of Kumani sometime tomorrow."

"What about all those village elders who escaped last night?" Shoshanna inquired. "They need to come to justice as well."

"Oh, I'm sure that anyone from the Eagles' Nest will be able to recognize those needing to go to prison in each of their villages," Galen assured her. "So what about you, Mendi? What are your plans? Staying here?"

"Well, yes. I thought Ms. Bina and Yona might need some extra help around their cabin." The other four exchanged glances while grinning. They had already come to that conclusion.

"Great idea, Mendi," Roany replied with a smirk. "I'm sure Yona is going to require some assistance for a while as she recovers."

Looking down at the little hand, still holding tight, Shoshanna bent over to speak with Eliam.

"And what are you planning to do, Eliam?"

"I don't know."

"Would you like to hang out with us for a while?" she inquired.

"Could I?" he asked excitedly.

"Well, of course you can, buddy!" Galen replied. "You can be our guide once we get back to Camp Shabelle. Is that okay with you?"

251

"Yes! I can show you all around!"

"Wonderful," Galen answered, heaving an exaggerated sigh of relief. "I don't know what we would do without you!"

Jessah smiled as she watched the sweet interactions they were having with her little friend. Seeing their gentleness reminded her of both Miss Haddie and Oren. She had grown quite fond of the two adults in her life and was actually feeling a little homesick to see them again.

"Well, rather than just talking about Camp Shabelle," Jessah suggested, "if you follow me, I can get all of us there in just a few steps."

"Okay, Jessah," Galen replied. "Lead on." Turning back towards Mendi, he added, "We'll probably see all of you tomorrow. Enjoy your day!"

"Okay. Thanks!" Happily, Mendi returned to two of his favorite friends awaiting him in the cabin.

With only a few steps, the entire group was immediately moved to the grounds outside Camp Shabelle where Uri happily played ball with a group of the boys. They kicked the ball back and forth as the children tried to steal the ball back for their own team.

Looking around, they spotted Oren, sitting underneath a tree with dozens of little girls gathered around him. They were all working on making crowns and chain necklaces, made with wildflowers, for each of them to wear. Oren had multiple wreaths on his head and around his neck, but was focusing more on assisting one little girl as they attempted to fix her broken crown.

The group approaching was a little shocked to find Oren happily playing with the girls. When he looked up, he was surprised to see them, and maybe just a little embarrassed. Shoshanna was the first to speak.

"I'm amazed," she admitted. "I was expecting to see you flustered with all these children, but here you sit playing with them."

"Well, when Uri and I figured out we had a mess of children to take care of, we got creative. I suddenly remembered how I used to make flower chains with you when you were little. We started working on them together. Of course, the girls gravitated to me. Uri recalled how he used to love playing ball when he was growing up. He found a ball in the bushes and started running around with most of the boys, as you can see. The children seem to be happy enough."

"And you seem quite content, yourself," Shoshanna remarked. "Seeing all this brings back some childhood memories I had forgotten about. Memories of when mom was still with us and when you were much happier."

"Shoshanna, a lot has happened in me since you left. Elemet and Chen have taught me how I can be happy again as either "the Woodsman" or as a playmate with little girls. I like it. I think you will like the new me as well."

"I think I will like the new you and, hopefully, you will like the more mature me as well."

At this point, Roany was feeling a little uncomfortable and gestured for Jessah to join him as he went to visit with

Uri and the boys, allowing Shoshanna, Galen, and Oren the personal time they needed. Oren continued, even as the little girls added fresh flowers behind his ears.

"And please tell me about this new mature, Shoshanna wearing a ring upon her finger and holding the hand of a little boy. I definitely want to know you better," Oren stated.

Suddenly Shoshanna remembered the man who had given her the ring.

"Oh yes! Father, do you remember Galen? You met him right before we…"

Oren completed her sentence for her. "…went running off into the woods to avoid the enforcers who were pursuing you. I certainly do remember! Hi Galen!" he said while extending his hand to him. "I see you were successful in protecting my daughter and now I see you have succeeded in winning her heart as well."

"Uh, yes. I guess I have," Galen responded, a little unsure of how to answer. "I would have certainly discussed this with you, but…"

"Yes, we were all in very challenging circumstances and locations at the time. We can get to know each other a little better now. I am, however, very good friends with your parents, Eber and Giza. That should encourage you."

"Yes, thank you!" Galen replied.

"So Shoshanna, you want to tell me about this little boy clinging to your hand?" Oren questioned her.

Looking down at the little boy's clear, hazel eyes and curly brown hair, Shoshanna's heart just melted inside her.

"Well, he's Jessah's friend, from the orphanage, and we just met. His name is Eliam and he hasn't let go of my hand since we first encountered each other." As an after-thought, she added, "Oh, and he is a very brave little boy! Really, he is a hero because he and Jessah prevented Yona's kidnapping."

"Really!" Oren leaned closer to Eliam. "May I shake the hand of a real hero?" he asked.

Eliam looked up quickly to check with Shoshanna. She smiled and nodded for him to let go and shake Oren's large hand. Eliam beamed with pride as he once again took hold of Shoshanna's hand.

"Not wanting to interrupt, sir," Galen asked, "but where is Miss Moselle and all the others supposedly taking care of all these children? Jessah told us a little about this ter-rible place."

"Well," Oren smiled, "from what I hear, they are still locked in the kitchen with the finest food you can imagine."

"Do you think it might be time for us to escort them someplace for safekeeping?" Galen asked, not wanting to appear overbearing in any way.

"Well, yes. I suppose it is probably time for them to be placed in a more secure location, like a prison. They have many things they will need to give an account for. Why don't we go and speak with Uri about that, especially since he has the only keys that will open the doors for them."

"And what about all these children?" Shoshanna asked.

""I think if we talk with the children first, explaining-what we are about to do, they will understand," her father responded. "I believe it is important for them to see that those who have neglected them will have to stand and give an answer for all their mistreatment."

With that, Oren stood and encouraged all the children to gather around so the adults could explain exactly what was going to happen. Once an explanation was given, Oren emphasized that they would never have to live in Camp Shabelle ever again, nor would they have to be afraid of Miss Moselle or any of the other staff.

"But who will be our parents?" one older boy asked.

"I don't know all the answers now," Oren replied, "but tomorrow, when Chen speaks, we will all hear together what he plans to do. We can relax, because he and his father, Elemet, are always good."

Though the children had many more questions, Oren and Uri encouraged them to have faith. They entered Camp Shabelle together to free their captors and then lead them to the closest prison where they would be held.

After the staff from Camp Shabelle were left at the prison, Shoshanna leaned over towards her father and whispered.

"And what are we going to do with all these hungry and tired children?"

Instead of answering her question, Oren asked her a question in return.

"And what did you experience on your journey to the Eagles' Nest?"

"We saw Elemet provide for us every time and for every need."

Oren smiled as he nodded in agreement. "Won't he do the same for all these precious children?"

Shoshanna knew her father was right.

They had only walked a short distance when Jessah spotted a bright light emanating from the forest.

"Head right towards it, my dear," Oren told her. "I'm sure that is where we all will be camping."

As promised, the children gasped in excitement as they discovered tents for every person and bountiful amounts of food, enough to fill every stomach. Eagerly, they all sat down together, feasting before retiring to their comfortable tents and bedding.

Tomorrow would certainly be a day they would never forget.

Chapter Thirty-Four

THE PLACE OF REST

A long and clear trumpet sounded across the land! Everyone who heard, understood the purpose of that call without a word of explanation. The day had come when all would be set into order once again. That which had been committed in darkness was now exposed and soon to be dealt with. A general assembly had been announced and all residents of the land were compelled by a deep desire to attend.

Men, women, and children traveled from everywhere to a large clearing near to what had been known as the smoking mountains. With the backdrop of a lush green and pristine alpine mountain behind them, a large platform was being assembled by craftsmen from the Eagles' Nest in preparation for the meeting the following day.

As the people arrived, tents were set up in circles all over the region with piles of firewood placed in the center so a comforting fire could be lit overnight. Beyond the camp-sites lay meadows filled with wildflowers where brooks with clear running, waters danced over the stones.

All things were prepared for the day of truth where peace and freedom would reign over Kumani once more.

Awakened by the trumpet blast, Oren opened his eyes. Though now awake, his mind was still playing back his dream where Dara, his deceased wife, was walking through a field of flowers surrounded by laughing children. Her smile was almost intoxicating as she lovingly stroked the hair and kissed the cheeks of the children around her. Suddenly, her face transformed into Shoshanna, his daughter. He watched as she leaned over and picked up a little boy running over to her. As she walked along with the child, a young man approached and put his arm around Shoshanna's waist. Together they walked away, happy and content.

As he considered his dream, he realized what he was seeing. This was Elemet's way of letting him know that just as he had to release his wife, he now must also release Shoshanna to live out the life Elemet had prepared for her. He knew this would not be easy.

"And what about me?" he quietly whispered. "Where will I find my place of joy here on Kumani?

He no sooner asked when Tanzi's face appeared before him. Her glistening black hair shone as her soft brown eyes gazed back at him. His heart was moved by her great humility and transparency while openly admitting her past deception before others. This formerly hardened woman had become soft and gentle as the love and forgiveness of Chen washed over her. He had even grown to admire her as she now freely gave to whoever was in need around her.

259

Yes, he might need to turn his attention towards Tanzi once everything settled down. And then he remembered… he had over fifty young children outside his tent needing his care! Immediately, he bolted upright pulling the flaps back on his tent.

Realizing only a few children had arisen, he sighed with relief and dressed himself quickly so as to oversee their breakfast. Shoshanna, Galen, and the other adults were getting up as well, so they sprang into action, making certain that every child had enough food, was properly clothed with two shoes on their feet, and ready to go.

As the adults busied themselves with their necessary preparations, Oren couldn't help but notice that young Eliam was still hanging onto Shoshanna's clothing as she hurried around assisting the other children.

"Yep," he thought to himself. "That little boy is a keeper for sure." He only hoped that Galen would feel the same about him as Shoshanna obviously did.

It didn't take too long for all the children to be assembled and prepared to make their journey towards the former smoking mountains.

With ten or so children assigned to each of the five adults, they had their hands quite full as the children laughed, played, and sometimes wandered off a little, while exploring the forest around them.

Shoshanna had already called upon her invisible warriors to help corral the children as they moved along. They were still somewhat visible to the children, so even the twelve stoic warriors would occasionally smile as some of the young boys would grab for their limbs hoping for either a ride upon their feet or be lifted into the air as they hung onto their massive arms.

These children were finally fearless and free.

After a long day of travel and not too many delays, the group arrived at the place where everyone was congregating. The children whooped playfully as they dashed through the meadow towards the camp grounds. The adults did their best to keep them at least in the general vicinity, but it was a challenge. Eventually, they settled on one camping area that would accommodate them all. As always, the food already awaited them and after their long hike, all of the travelers were tired and ready for a break — especially the adults!

Once their stomachs were full, the children settled down nicely, enjoying the comfortable fire as they rested their tired bodies. Jessah, however, was not quite ready to end her day, so she decided to wander among all the surrounding campsites just to see who she might run into. After assuring both Oren and Shoshanna that she would be back before too long, she chose to walk along the peripheries of the camps. Looking around, Jessah could see the mosaic of people from all the island regions, enjoying one another. While they visited, dancing flames of fire cast ever-changing shadows on the ground.

With all the busy excitement the last few days, Jessah found herself longing for periods of the peace and quiet she had experienced at her home with Miss Haddie. She had forgotten how busy and active children can be. By spending so much of her time around adults, she realized she had begun to pick some of their quiet ways—and besides, she was rapidly approaching her eleventh birthday!

"I'm not really a child, but nearly a preteen," she told herself. While pondering her tween state of maturity, she suddenly noticed that she was no longer walking alone. She looked up to see someone she had only seen in her dreams. Elemet!

"You have done well, Jessah," Elemet smiled. In an instant, Jessah was no longer walking the outskirts of the campsite, but had been moved to a pinnacle on the former smoking mountains overlooking the massive meadow below. The entire scene now looked more like a massive quilt with white tents and blazing fires at the center of each patchwork with men, women, and children milling around as the sun began dipping down behind the mountains. The view left her awestruck and quite without words for a time.

"So, is this what you see?" she asked, while still studying the view below.

"This is only a small part of what I see," he responded. "Not only do I see the big picture of the present, but I also see the past, and the future as well. I see every particle of life found within every individual on Kumani. I created them in hopes that they would choose to recognize and grow to love the source of all life—me."

Jessah looked up into his eyes of swirling eternity and innocently stated the obvious. "But not everyone has chosen to do that, have they?"

"No, unfortunately, not everyone has chosen the truth. This saddens me, but I am still hopeful that they will change their minds. When they let go of the lies they have embraced, I am able to heal and restore them."

"Are you talking about people like Cobar and Zelig? That was a terrible thing they were trying to do to Yona."

"Yes, that was a terrible thing," Elemet agreed, "but look how I was able to use you to stop them from getting away with that. You were very brave!"

"Thank you! Eliam was quite brave as well, wasn't he?"

"He sure was! Just you wait to see what that little boy becomes when he grows up! I have wonderful plans for him!"

Jessah smiled as she saw some mental pictures of Eliam accomplishing amazing things on the island of Kumani.

"Wow! That is going to be so exciting to see!" she agreed. But something was still bothering her. "So what are you going to do about people like Cobar and Zelig?"

"The same thing I do with all my people. I cause them to face the truth. They must choose for themselves if they will humbly acknowledge their deception and ask me for grace or choose to continue hiding in their shame. Choosing shame and guilt will lead to their ultimate destruction, something I have never desired for them," Elemet explained. "Tomorrow we will see what they choose."

Jessah dropped her head a little saying, "I feel sorry for those who have never found out how good and loving you are, but whatever they decide, I want you to know, I am choosing you."

Turning towards Elemet, Jessah wrapped her arms around him burying her face into the folds of his garments.

The sweetness of his fragrance filled her senses, causing her to completely forget where she was. As she floated in his love, she suddenly awakened to find herself in her own tent, back at the campsite.

Peeking out the flap of the tent, she realized that everyone had gone to bed. The flames of their fire pit had already diminished to nothing but glowing embers. For a brief second, she wondered if her encounter with Elemet had been real or just a dream, but as she took a breath, she could still smell the fragrances of the one she loved. Others might not believe her if she tried to explain what had happened, but none of that mattered. She knew. Contentedly, she laid her head back into her bedding and quickly fell into a blissful sleep.

Chapter Thirty-Five

COMING TO TERMS

Early the following morning, a final, long, trumpet blasted across the island, announcing the beginning of a new day and awakening the people of Kumani. Once breakfast had been eaten, the people began slowly moving towards the central stage to begin the meeting to which they had been called. Before they got too close to the platform, shrill calls of the giant, golden eagles filled the air above them.

The people gasped in amazement as they saw dozens of these great birds circling above with their huge wings extended. Slowly, the eagles began spiraling downward, closer and closer to the ground, until they landed upon the grass directly in front of the stage. One by one, the aerial warriors, including Azriel, slid off the backs of their birds and solemnly walked up the stairs leading to the platform. They stood at attention, awaiting the arrival of one they had all been waiting for. Chen!

Once again, another golden eagle, much bigger in size, appeared in the air above the crowd, slowly making its descent and gracefully landing upon the grass. Chen, himself, slid off his back, making his way up the stairs to center stage. Brilliant lights flashed all around him as his full regal attire reflected the sunlight in every direction.

The aerial warriors bowed respectfully as he passed by them to stand in front of the podium to address the people before him. However, before he began, there was one more entrance which caused quite a stir among the residents of the Eagles' Nest. They immediately recognized the aging woman and her sister approaching the platform, assisted by Yona and Mendi, who helped guide them along. The crowd respectfully parted, allowing the two sisters to walk up to a region directly in the front.

Whispers could be heard reverberating across the field.

"It's Miss Haddie and her sister Ms. Bina!" the residents informed the others.

Once Jessah spotted Miss Haddie, she came running up to join her in front. Miss Haddie reached over to hug the young girl.

"There is light all over you, child," she commented.

"I had an encounter last night," Jessah explained. "I'll tell you all about it later."

"I can't wait!" Miss Haddie replied.

Once the elder women were in place, Chen began speaking.

"Good morning, my dear friends. As you all know, we have been through a terrible siege on this island, one that has resulted in the loss of life, the loss of homes, and most saddening, the loss of freedom for a time. But that era has come to an end, thanks to the brave efforts of those willing to risk it all for a cause much bigger than themselves. Some of our heroes survived and some are already receiving their just rewards in a place where my father, Elemet resides."

"For those still in our midst, I want to honor them publicly. The men now standing with me on this platform—our aerial warriors—faced great risk to help end the reign of fear and control doming from Camp Coshek," Chen said, while gesturing towards the men standing behind him.

The crowd broke into applause as the warriors humbly bowed their heads before the people while Chen proceeded.

"There are many more heroes I could take the time to name, but there are several individuals, in particular, I would like to mention before moving onto the real purpose of this gathering. She has great repute among those already walking the ways of the eagle and submitting to my father and me. Some of you may not know her, but we know her well. She is known as Miss Haddie, a mentor, teacher, and encourager of many of our heroes. If you have not yet met her, I encourage you to listen to her wisdom when you have a chance, for she has learned much over the years."

Once again, applause filled the meadow as Miss Haddie blushed at all the attention she was getting.

When the applause subsided, Chen proceeded to honor and thank many of the warriors in the battle against darkness including Azriel, Galen, Shoshanna, Roany, Uri, Mendi, Oren, and even Ms. Bina was mentioned in his appreciation for their efforts in overcoming the control of fear.

"There are other valiant warriors I have yet to mention that some of you might have a tendency to overlook, but before I tell about them, we must deal with some important business regarding the freedom of every individual living here on Kumani," Chen continued.

"I would like every person who once served as an enforcer or informant, whether willingly or against your will, to please stand and walk to the front."

Slowly, different individuals arose from among their peers and family, moving to stand before Chen. Included in the crowd were both Mendi and Tanzi. Unsure of what might happen to those who once assisted the village elders in their control of the villages, most of those standing before Chen fully expected judgment to fall. Chen first exhorted them to all look at him.

As they lifted their heads and stared into his eyes, something appeared to hold their gaze so they could not look away. Though Tanzi had once sat in his presence, in her blindness, she had not seen the beauty of his penetrating eyes as they searched the very depths of her soul, revealing all buried guilt and shame which yet lingered. Mendi also was mesmerized by the love of this man who knew and understood everything about him, as a fiery passion washed over him.

Some people cried, some laughed, and some simply fell over as the guilt and shame left their minds. The surrounding crowd watched in awe as those once perceived as enemies, were set free and transformed before them. A sense of great peace settled over all as their souls were completely restored. When they could walk, many had to be assisted back to their families and friends. Once this was completed, Chen asked for all those who had yielded to the fear and control propagated by the village elders to simply raise their hands. Nearly every hand across the assembly went up.

With all eyes upon Chen, they watched as he simply blew over the entire group. Instantly, a gentle breeze moved across the crowd as fear was released from them all. Raising his hands, he then sent another wave of peace and joy over every individual. Again, emotions were stirred as they felt the residue of the fear vanish from their hearts and souls.

Eber and Giza, who were among the crowd, also felt the breeze, refreshing them both from all the busyness of serving the refugees they had housed. Eber, leaning over to Giza, remarked that he felt as though he had had a bath on the inside.

"I know!" his wife replied. "How does he do that?"

"I don't know how he does it, but I'm so glad he does. I feel so refreshed," Eber stated.

Seeing the freedom of the residents before him, Chen knew it was now time to test the refreshing they had all received. Calling for the prison guards to bring all of the captured village elders before the assembly, he watched as some of the villagers' faces turned from joy to anger as the handcuffed men were brought before the people. Cobar and Zelig stood out among the prisoners.

Yona, Ms. Bina, and even Jessah scowled at the two men who had caused so much pain and suffering. As the former village elders stood, broken and in chains before the people, Chen spoke up.

"What you see before you are men who allowed the deception of power and control to completely overtake them for a season. To fully understand how each of them arrived at this point in their lives, you would have to see them as I see them, from their very beginning to now. These men have admitted their own faults and deception as I sat and spoke with them. They have asked me to forgive them and now they ask if each of you would forgive them as well."

"Before you answer, let me remind you that each of you has been forgiven of many offenses as well, including the fears that you surrendered to recently. As I released you of your fears, I ask that you now release these men from their offenses as well. Though I have forgiven them, they have agreed to place themselves under house arrest as they submit to the teaching of Miss Haddie for an extended time. When she feels they are ready to join us, they will be released, one at a time."

As Chen's eyes scanned over the crowd, everyone felt him look right through them, and then he continued.

"It is my hope that when they are released, you will greet them as the long, lost brothers they each are and welcome them as you would welcome me. If you agree to this, I ask you to raise your hands."

As hands went up all over the meadow, Chen nodded and applauded the residents in their willingness to give their wayward brothers another chance at a productive life on Kumani. As the men were escorted out, there was one more person Chen needed to bring before the people. Hamah.

The crowd watched as this man was paraded before them, handcuffed and wearing chains around his ankles. Slowly, he shuffled his way up to the front escorted by Chen's personal warriors, now visible before the crowd.

Though most of the people had no idea who he was, Oren, Mendi, Shoshanna, Galen, and Roany were very aware of who he was. Every eye followed his progress to the front. Once he was in position, Chen began.

"I bring before you the man responsible for not only prolonging the effects of the haze over the lowlands of Kumani. He is also the one who destroyed many lives and drugged dissenters forcing them to act upon his bidding alone. Through him, we saw the complete destruction of Yashen and many of its residents."

As the people looked upon Hamah, they saw no remorse, only a stony expression as he looked downward, avoiding all eye contact. He clearly had refused the love and kindness extended to him by Chen.

"Because I am concerned about each of you, I ask you to release and forgive this man for all his wickedness so that you will not be crippled in your new-found freedom. Though he has yet to respond to my love, there is still time when he may turn and discover the true life he was created for. However, until that time, some of my warriors will keep him confined in a secure facility in the Eagles' Nest. My question to you is, will you choose to forgive him and even have mercy upon him in your own hearts just as you did with the village elders? If you are willing to forgive him, please raise your hands."

Once again, every hand rose in agreement with what Chen was asking. Chen smiled at the crowds before him as he signaled his warriors to escort Hamah away to confinement. With that now complete, Chen announced that he had one more matter he needed to address.

"If you recall, I spoke of some other valiant warriors I would like to honor before you. At this time I would like all the children of Camp Shabelle to come join me on the stage…and that would include our friend, Jessah as well."

Shocked, Jessah looked up at Miss Haddie.

"Go ahead, child," she encouraged her. "Chen has asked for you."

A little shaken at her name being called from the platform, Jessah joined all the other children as they stepped up the stairs and stood beside Chen, facing the crowd. Chen proceeded.

"As you look upon all these young faces, I want to remind you that each of these children were separated from their parents, having to endure very difficult circumstances in Camp Shabelle. Under the care of Miss Moselle and others, they were unfortunately, neglected and forcibly trained to submit to all the deceptions of the village elders and their ways."

Then turning towards the children, Chen addressed them as he motioned for one more group of people to be brought before them. As he began his words of instruction, Miss Moselle and her staff were brought to the front, also in handcuffs. Uri couldn't help but smile a little as he saw their handcuffs. Instead of facing the crowd, Chen had the staff of Camp Shabelle face the children.

"Children, what you see here are some very fearful and hurting people who unfortunately worked against you. They attempted to control you with lies. They will be corrected and retrained so they will no longer hurt others. But my concern is for you. Rather than carrying your painful past with you throughout your lives, I ask that you forgive and release these people so that you can be free. Will you do that?" Chen asked them.

All the children responded that they would forgive them. Once that was done, Chen announced to the crowd that they would also be sent to Miss Haddie for further healing and instruction. As the group was escorted away, Chen then called Jessah and little Eliam to come stand beside him.

Nervously, Jessah grabbed Eliam's hand and the two of them stood beside Chen. Understanding their nervousness, Chen gently laid his hands upon both children as he spoke on their behalves.

"Though you may look upon these young ones as simply children, I want to tell you that both these children have fearlessly walked before those we might call their enemies. However, because of their trust in Elemet, they were able to move freely and boldly to accomplish everything they were asked to do. Jessah has been visiting Camp Shabelle at night instructing the children in the ways of the eagle and preparing them for their freedom, which Uri assisted with. Thank you, Uri!"

"But beyond that, both young Eliam and Jessah boldly stood before some men planning to take something that was not theirs to take. Even when they were threatened with bodily harm, they did not move. They stood their ground until help arrived. Consequently, one young woman is now safe and free, thanks to their courage. Would you join me in honoring these children?"

As the crowd excitedly applauded, Jessah looked up into Chen's eyes. She suddenly realized that his eyes were swirling with the same blue eternity she had seen in Elemet's eyes. The love of both the father and the son now washed over her in one moment. It was nearly more than she could endure, but somehow she managed to stand. With great compassion, Chen looked over the crowd and made his final appeal.

"While you look at all these children standing here, there will be some of you feeling an impulse to gather up one of these former orphans and open your home to include them in your family. It is my desire that not one of these children be left without a real home and parents who love them. In caring for these children, you will find your own care and provision flowing into your homes as you learn more about the ways of the eagle and come to know my father, Elemet."

"There are many people already among who can help you discover the joys in flying high with the eagles far above all the cares and worries of this life. You are invited to learn more so you may truly live and prosper. Go now in peace as your families are restored to you."

With joyful celebration, the people began spontaneously hugging one another. What a day it had been! Some of the crowd jubilantly searched for some of the heroes Chen had mentioned. Galen and Shoshanna found themselves surrounded by grateful villagers, thanking them for the part they had played. As they pressed forward towards the stage, Eliam came running up to them, excitedly reporting how Chen had said his name. Galen picked up the boy and hugged him as Shoshanna watched. Whispering into his ear, Eliam turned towards Shoshanna and asked her something.

"Galen wants to know if you are ready to marry him and adopt me now?"

Tears ran down her face as she hugged both Galen and Eliam. "The answer is 'yes,'" she responded.

As Pacey and young Lahela watched all the happy mayhem around them, Pacey reminded her daughter that they would be just fine. Suddenly, her eyes spotted someone who looked familiar moving towards them. With his arm still in a sling, Jovan maneuvered as quickly as he could towards the family he had been taken away from. Pacey screamed in excitement as she rushed to his side with Lahela following close behind.

"I can't believe it is you!" she cried as tears of joy ran down her cheeks.

"It's me, alright. It's been a long trip to finally come back to you both. I love you so much!" he said as they kissed with Lahela jubilantly hugging both her parents.

People from all over the meadow rushed up to the stage, asking the various children if they would like to join their families. Of course, the children eagerly responded to the invitations. This continued until only Jessah remained on the stage, still standing next to Chen as she happily watched all the celebrations occurring across the meadow.

Jessah scanned the crowd looking for Miss Haddie. She finally spotted her, but with so many people surrounding and wanting to speak with the celebrated mentor, Jessah could see she was quite busy. Trying not to let loneliness enter in, Jessah decided she had better just walk off the stage herself. However, before she got very far, Chen leaned over and whispered something in her ear that made her eyes grow wide in wonder.

Hurriedly, she moved towards the steps to get down, but before she took her last step, Oren and Tanzi stood before her with a huge grin on both their faces. She looked at them quite puzzled.

"So Jessah, it sounds like Miss Haddie is going to be quite busy now." Oren said.

"Yes, that's probably true, but I'll be fine," Jessah assured him.

"You probably would be fine, but I thought I might just suggest another option."

"And what is that?" she asked.

"How about if you join Tanzi and me in being a real family?" he said with a smile. "I've gotten quite used to seeing you rather frequently. Shoshanna is obviously growing up and developing a family of her own, so I thought, why not? You could still go see Miss Haddie any time you wanted. What do you think?"

After looking back and forth between the happy couple, she responded.

"Why not? That sounds great! Could I call you mom and dad?"

"I would love that!" Oren replied. "What do you think, Tanzi?"

"I would be so honored to have you as a daughter!" the woman said happily. "I've never had a daughter before, so you'll have to help me figure this out."

"Oh, I can do that!" Jessah smiled. "Would it be alright if we discuss this further in just a little bit? I have an important appointment I need to take care of. Okay?"

"Sure, but where are you off to?" Oren asked.

"Oh, you'll see!" she answered. "Chen sent me on a little mission."

As Oren and Tanzi watched, Jessah rushed over towards all the golden eagles who still remained off to the side of the platform. A great number of people had assembled around the amazing birds, curiously looking them over, but were too nervous to approach them. Jessah, however, had no hesitation whatsoever as she moved through the crowd.

It only took a moment for her to spot the largest and most magnificent of all the golden eagles.

"Goldie!" she called out. Immediately the great bird flapped his wings in excitement to see one of his favorite riders approaching him. Lovingly, she stroked his elegant, golden feathers and gazed into his eyes.

"Are you ready to go flying?" The eagle quickly lowered one of his wings so Jessah could step up and plant herself upon his back. "Let's go!" she shouted as the eagle stretched out his massive wings and lit into the air. Looking down below her, she spotted Oren and Tanzi and directed Goldie to swoop down close by them so she could say hi.

"Woohoo!" she shouted at them. "Look at me!"

Tanzi had her mouth open as she watched the fearless child fly far above them. She looked at Oren to see what he had to say.

"This might not be as easy as I thought," he admitted to Tanzi, shirking his shoulders as he looked upward again. "We'll figure it out."

OTHER BOOKS WRITTEN BY MARY TRASK

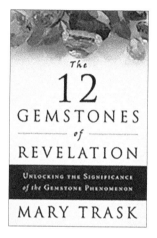

Also available at:

www.heartreflectionsministries.com

CPSIA information can be obtained
at www.ICGtesting.com
Printed in the USA
FFHW020059311019
55885783-61766FF